CLAIMED BY NIGHT

THE QUEEN'S CONSORTS: BOOK 1

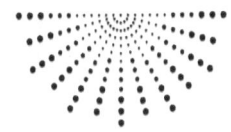

ELENA LAWSON

GET MORE

Join the author's New Releases mailing list and be the first to know when they release a new book. You'll also receive exclusive updates, sneak peaks and freebies.
Visit *www.leamckee.com* to get started.

CHAPTER ONE

The water beckoned, wild and dark, undulating in the crisp moonlight. Thana kept close to my side as we traveled the winding path to the shore. There the envoy waited, ready with a ship meant to carry me away from this lonely place. It heaved on the back of the midnight tide, a polished black beast with silver sails.

The queen is dead.

I was told the Night Court is grief-stricken and in shock at the abrupt end of Enya. But those were emotions I couldn't bring myself to feel for the female who bore me. I knew her face only from the tapestry hung in the temple on the hill, but I had never heard her voice, felt her touch—had never *known her*. Spirited away to the Isle of Mist as an infant, I'd seen nothing outside this place. Thana, my handmaiden, and the seven females who tend to the isle were the only family—*the only other Fae*—I had ever known.

Thana folded my arm into hers as we neared the males gathered beside a smaller vessel nestled between the pebbles at the edge of the water. "Chin up, Liana," Thana whispered, giving my hand a reassuring squeeze, "Never let them think you're weak

1

or they'll eat you up and spit you out. You are their queen, now you must act the part."

I nodded my understanding, attempted to make my eyes harder, my jawline stronger.

"Your Majesty." The male closest to us stepped forward, bending at the middle in a small bow, "I am Captain of the Queen's Guard. It is my honor to ferry you home." His face was half concealed in shadow, but I could see his tired eyes, thick unibrow, and a face that was unshaven and rounded. The captain's voice was brusque, and he wreaked of cloves and seafoam.

So, this is a male... How disappointing.

The other four remained still behind their master, hooded and cloaked.

"Your name?" I asked him.

"Ronan, Your Majesty. My sword is yours as it was your mother's."

I stepped past his outstretched hand, stifling the urge to snicker at him, "A lot of good that did her, *captain*. Shall we?"

I didn't wait for his reply, stepping past the cloaked sentries and into the small boat, Thana on my heels. I said a farewell to the others this morning, with a promise I would return when I could, with gifts for each of them. They wouldn't be joining me at court. The island has been their home for nearly a millennium, they now belong to it, and it to them.

But Thana, *my* Thana, had only been on the isle since I arrived as a babe, entrusted to watch over me these past twenty-three years. She was the only one able to leave and return, departing at the beginning of each moon cycle to gather supplies, and returning in days with a bounty of grain, cloth, and other necessities. I expected to wait at least a century before I could get off the damned rock, but fate, it seemed had other plans.

I only just began my immortal life one year past. Thana

didn't begin her immortal life until she was twenty-eight. The others on the island all at varying ages from twenty to thirty-three. It was like waking up. As though I'd been underwater all that time and had only then been able to breech the surface—to truly breathe. And it was cold, like a fist of ice curling its talons around my heart, shooting frigid water through my veins. In the days following, everything became clearer. My senses sharpened, and my reflexes were faster. Even my skin and hair grew softer.

But the people knew. The denizens of the Night Court would balk at my age. I would be the youngest queen to take power since the reign of Morgana two thousand years ago. They still sang songs about her greatness. Perhaps one day, they would have songs to remember me. If I survived long enough.

They told us Enya was assassinated. It was the only explanation. They found her in her chambers, fingers curled inwards, eyes bloodshot, her skin a pallid blue. Poison, they said. But how it got past her food tasters is a mystery. From the symptoms, they suspect it was verbane berries.

I *dared* someone to try the same poison on me. Verbane berries grew wild all over the Isle of Mist and I'd been eating them since I was a child. They almost killed me a few times before the seven sisters realized why I was constantly taking ill and warned me away from them. But I hadn't died from them, and I liked the taste, so I ate one a day until my stomach didn't turn anymore, and then a few a day after that. Eventually, I could eat as many as a handful without too painful of side-effects.

The small boat bobbed and rocked on the water as the four hooded males paddled us out. I watched as the Isle of Mist became smaller, the only sign of life a flickering light where the temple stood at the crest of the tallest hill. I wouldn't miss it. It was a cage, the kind meant to keep you safe, not hold you prisoner, but some days—*most days*, it felt more like the latter.

Movement in the water caught my eye.

A flicker of glowing blue darted under the boat, another chasing it through the inky blackness of the depths. I leaned over the side, watching the wraiths below. Devious creatures, bound to no one, they served only themselves. I'd never seen one before and thought they lived closer to the shore, in tidal pools and underwater caves. *They shouldn't be this far out to sea.*

"Don't get too close to the edge, Your Majesty," the sentry sitting next to me said, peeking up from under his hood. A set of eyes glinted in the moonlight, steel blue, and piercing, in a face that seemed chiseled from stone. I was so busy admiring him, I didn't have time to react when a tendril of cold, wet tentacle wrapped around my wrist.

The last thing I heard was Thana's shout as my body flew from the boat, crashing into the sea. My lungs constricted, the cold of the water seeping into my bones. I yanked at the tentacle around my wrist, but it was no use. The wraith pulled me down into the dark until the pressure was enough to squeeze the air from my lungs.

This would *not* be my end. I remembered the dagger at my thigh and tried to yank it free of its leather holster. The water became alive with shimmering blue and silver. They surrounded me. Their sharp-angled ethereal faces snarled and hissed, their glowing white eyes fixed on me.

Come with us... Their raspy song-like voices sang inside my mind. *Come...*

A tentacle whipped out to snatch the dagger from my fingertips, but that same tentacle was then severed, the wraith emitting a hair-raising shriek. A dark shape came into view, brandishing a longsword. He grabbed me, slicing the head from the wraith who held me, her glowing blue light flickering, and then fading. The wraiths scattered further into the deep as we rose, his arm around my waist, hauling me toward the rippling surface.

We broke through, me sputtering and coughing at the warm night air rushing to fill my emptied lungs. Strong arms pulled me back into the boat where Thana wrapped her thin cloak around me, "You stupid, stupid girl. What were you thinking?" she shrieked as the male who saved me hauled himself back into the boat.

"That is no way to speak to your queen!" the captain shouted, and I turned to find him seated and dry, his sword still in its scabbard. *Then who...*

"Silence," I commanded him, earning myself a pained scowl. It was the male still standing who drew my attention.

The male unclasped his cloak, letting it fall into a wet heap around him. His voice was husky as he said, "Are you alright, Your Majesty?"

Another of the males whispered to his companion, "The wraiths wouldn't dare disrupt a royal vessel, much less attack..."

"Something isn't right. The wraiths are a peaceful creature."

Then the captain, "We must make haste, lest the beasts return."

The male with eyes of steel resumed his position next to me, dripping wet. He met my gaze for only an instant before taking up his oar and begging to paddle with the other three.

The sensation returned to my fingers, Thana's cloak and her hands working to rub warmth back into me. "Thank you, sir," I said to the male next to me, his water dampened skin rippling with flexed muscle at each stroke of his oar.

He offered me one terse nod, his dark hair falling into his face. "Alaric, majesty. You may call me Alaric."

As we climbed the ladder onto the larger vessel and sailed away, the mist shrouding the island from the rest of Meloran swallowed us up and spat us back out on the other side. The island evaporated as though it was a figment of my imagination. They say the Isle of Mist could only be found by those who knew exactly where to look. And until her assassination, the only person outside of it who knew its whereabouts was my mother. Its location was marked on a map, sealed by Enya herself, only to be opened in the event of her death.

Once out of the mist, the isle disappeared completely. I breathed a sigh. Of relief? Of sadness? I wasn't sure.

It would be two days before we saw the shores of Meloran and I took my place at the Night Court. Three more days from then and I would complete the Blessing Ceremony and receive my Grace from the Fae who came before us. Thana was Graced with air, and it was her who coaxed the wind into our sails. She thought mine would be tied to water, for the stormy blue of my eyes, or light—for the shinning silver of my long hair, but I believed my Grace would be drawn of shadow, for the darkness surrounding my heart. I didn't much care what it would be, only that I received one. A queen without a Grace was not one fit to rule.

I stood at the stern of the ship, keeping my eyes fixed to the horizon, searching for the first signs of land. From a cage of stones and mist to one of gold and sentries. At least it would be a change, and hopefully an improvement.

CHAPTER TWO

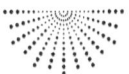

"*D*rink it, Liana. It will quell the feeling," Thana said, trying *again* to push the mug into my hands.

I moaned, shoving the mug back at her, the yellowish liquid splashing to the floor. "Just get me off this *damned* boat!"

I wasn't sure if it was the boat's fault or the nerves. By tomorrow we'd be docking on the shores of the Night Court and I didn't know what to expect—how the people would react. It didn't help that Thana brought up my birth father. Still living, Edris was acting as King Regent until my return.

The moment I landed on the continent, the power would fall into my hands, as it had fallen into the hands of each female before me. There hadn't been a king in power for an age, not since the Mad King brought destruction to our lands. It was his daughter, Morgana, who brought back peace and decreed that the crown should pass to her first-born female heir with full council support. It had been that way ever since. I didn't care to meet Edris. He left me on that damned rock, the same as my mother.

He didn't deserve my respect. And he wouldn't get it.

Thana rolled her eyes at me for the hundredth time, "I don't know why you always have to be so difficult."

"I don't know why *you*—"

"Excuse me, milady, majesty, may I be of assistance? The captain heard shouting."

I looked up to find Alaric standing in the doorway of my quarters and groaned again, "No. Thank you, Alari—"

"She's seasick," Thana said in a huff, standing to fetch more of her putrid tea mixture from the bedside table, "And moody as the gods."

Alaric stepped into the room, no longer cloaked, but wearing his sentry armor. Glimmering black offset the tan gold of his skin and the blue-silver of his eyes. *Stop it, Lianna. Just because you've never seen a male before doesn't mean you need to go drooling over the first one you see... even if he is the most beautiful creature you've ever seen.*

"I may be able to alleviate it."

I wanted to tell him he already was, standing there being so distracting and all, but instead I nodded.

Thana tossed the mug onto the nightstand, stomping from the room with a shake of her head. "Knows me her entire life and won't accept *my* help, oh *no*, but a pretty male she's only just met—why of course!" she grumbled, her voice growing further away as she stormed through the bowels of the ship.

"May I," Alaric asked, gesturing to the vacant spot next to me on the bed. The covers were strewn all over and I was laying in a massive pile of pillows, my hair sticking to my neck and temples. I hadn't thought of how I must look, and rushed to push my hair back and rub the sleep out of my eyes as Alaric sat next to me.

He met my gaze with an unwavering one of his own. I was the first to avert my eyes as he said, "May I see your hand?"

I cocked my head at him, eyes squinting, but I gave him my

hand nonetheless, ready to be rid of the nausea, "Is this some sort of sailor's trick?"

He shook his head, a small smirk turning up the corners of his lips, "No, majesty, it's something I learned long ago."

He gathered my hand into his own, holding it palm-up. I attempted to hide the shiver running up my spine when he traced a line down my palm with his other hand. He then pressed firmly on a spot a few fingers width from my wrist on my forearm, deftly avoiding where the wraith's tentacle left an angry red mark on my wrist—though it had already faded and didn't hurt anymore.

There we sat in silence for what seemed an hour but could only have been a few moments, and then, "There," he said, letting go of my arm and setting my hand into my lap.

I gingerly touched the spot he was holding, a phantom pressure still lingering there. Then I realized, my eyes widening as my hand flew to my stomach, "How?" I asked, incredulous. The nausea was gone, replaced with a ravenous hunger I hadn't felt for the better part of two days.

Alaric shrugged, moving to stand, "I'm glad you're feeling better, Your Majesty."

"Liana." I corrected, "We aren't even at court yet and I'm already tired of all the formality."

"I couldn't possibly," he stuttered, a note of worry in his words, "My captain would have my head."

My dressing robe came off the post of my bed with a sharp tug. I stood next to him, wrapping the light material over my undergarments—not realizing until it was too late that it's improper for a lady to be undressed in front of anyone but her handmaidens. *Damn all these rules! How am I ever to remember them all?* They could have thrown a few males onto that rock in the middle of the sea with me if only so I'd have learned how to behave in front of them.

"When we're alone then," I said, immediately regretting the

words. *When we're alone? Why should we have any reason to be alone together ever again? Stupid.* Thana was right, I would be a disaster of a queen.

He cleared his throat, doing his absolute best to avert his gaze as I finished tying the dressing robe. "Yes, your maj—er, Liana. It would be my honor." He moved to the doorway, and I was about to thank him for his help when he turned, "It's best to be outside, to quell the seasickness. Meloran will be on the horizon at dawn. If you'd like, I can send word when it's within our sights."

"Yes. I would like that."

MELORAN. The land stretched on as far as my eyes could see in either direction. To the north lay the Wastes, and even with the distance I could see the mountainous landscape, and how the sun—though it shone brightly on us, didn't dare touch it. It was where the first Fae settled, and was the original Night Court until it fell to ruin under the rule of the Mad King some millennia ago.

To the south lay the realm of the Day Court, our perpetual adversaries, though I couldn't understand why. Sure, there was a war between courts a thousand years ago, but that was then. This is now. With my Fae eyes, I could see how the trees seemed greener, how the sunlight played on the water near their shores, making it seem more transparent, almost turquoise.

And ahead, cast in both shadow and light, lay the Night Court. *My court.* I watched, transfixed, as we drew nearer. The palace came into view after a short time, its spires, towers, and walkways all seemed hewn from the stars themselves and shone like polished ivory against the dark stone of the cliffside. It was beyond anything I could've imagined, and even more beautiful than how Thana described it.

"Your Majesty, I present to you your kingdom." The Captain

of the Queen's Guard came to stand beside me at the bow, "It must seem vast compared to the Isle of Mist."

Yes, I thought, *remind me I've spent the entirety of my life trapped on an all but deserted island as if I'd forgotten.* I did not give him the courtesy of a response, turning instead to where Thana waited to escort me below deck. It was time to get ready, as she kept reminding me, I couldn't be seen wearing trousers outside of the ship. She shrieked when she beheld me wearing them, ordering me to remove them at once. I'd always preferred trousers and simple blouses to skirts and gowns. On the isle, I could wear what I liked. It seemed now, I didn't have a say in even that.

"You're a fast learner," I mused as Thana braided and twisted my hair into an elaborate crown-like shape on top of my head. I watched her reflection in the mirror raise an eyebrow in question, "Do you know how long Alaric has been a member of the Queen's Guard?"

She pulled my hair tighter, her lips pursed, "Taken a liking to him, have you?"

I shrugged.

"He's brand new, all of them are save for the captain."

I moved to face her, but she tugged my head back into place by my hair, "All?" I asked, allowing her to finish sticking pins into my skull, "Why were they all replaced?"

She inhaled slowly, considering, "The captain had reason to believe they were involved in the assassination of Enya, so, he banished them. But don't worry dear, the new sentries have extensive training. He hand selected three of them and the council selected the fourth as is custom. Your *Alaric* was second in command to the Captain of the Horde."

The Horde? He didn't seem like the warrior type—in looks maybe, with his wide chest and corded muscle, but not in any other way I'd think a member of our armies to be.

Thana draped a delicate strand of black diamonds around

my neck and stepped back to admire her handiwork, smiling one of her rare smiles, "There. You're stunning."

I shook my head at her, unconcerned with my appearance. "Send word to the council members when we arrive. I'd like to meet with them. Tonight."

THE MOOD at the palace was a far cry from that of the towns-folk. When we disembarked from the ship at sunset, an energetic crowd met us with cheers and shouts. They were joyous and stumbling over one another to welcome me home and give me their well wishes. With Alaric on one side of me, the captain on the other, and the other three sentries and Thana flanking us, none of them tried to get too close. *But they were my people, shouldn't I feel safe among them?* They were, after all, ungraced, and therefore posed little threat.

"Welcome home, Your Majesty," a groundskeeper said as we entered the palace gardens and I thanked her quietly, taking in the grandeur of the foliage surrounding us. There were flowers the size of my head, and some as tiny as a breadcrumb. And colors, so many colors—*and smells.* Heady smells that tickled my nose gave a sense of calm.

I was glad there was no applause there, nor any sort of welcome. It was a place of peaceful solitude, and I liked it that way.

On the other side of the gardens lay a marble-arched hallway connecting one wing of the palace to the other. Thana took the lead, steering us towards the western wing. On entering the mass of hewn stone, she turned on her heel to face the captain and his sentries, "Liana is in need of rest, I will escort her to her quarters."

The captain looked taken aback at the subtle command in Thana's words, "I cannot allow the queen to be unattended, even within the walls of the palace. I will accompany you."

"You will not," the words squeaked past my lips before I could stop them, "I mean, am I not safe in my palace, or are you that terrible at your job, captain?" *And there I go again...* I could almost hear Thana's chastising voice in my head, *patience, integrity, loyalty, and honesty, those are the traits of a great leader, not pig-headedness and pride.*

He had the sense to remain silent for an instant before he said, "With the recent assassination of the late queen—gods rest her eternal soul—I would think it wise to stay with you at all times. Wouldn't you agree, Thana?"

Using Thana's love for me as leverage. What a manipulative ass. "Fine," I said before Thana could answer him, "Perhaps you're right and it would be wise to have someone well trained, equipped, and *trustworthy* to protect me at my side."

The captain nodded his agreement, shifting a foot forward to follow. I held up a hand, meeting his confused stare. "Alaric will escort me."

"But, Your Majesty, I—" the captain started, but I held up my hand again to silence him, catching the slight widening of Alaric's eyes, and the tightening of his jaw.

"My decision is final," I said, waiting for Alaric to move into place at my side before following a tense Thana from the foyer. I called back over my shoulder, "I will see you tonight, captain, at the council meeting."

CHAPTER THREE

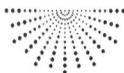

We'd encountered few others walking the halls and corridors of the palace, and I was grateful because it gave me time to admire its stunning architecture. The palace was built under the reign of Morgana, and I had to admit, she had great taste. There wasn't a single thing about it I would change. As we rounded a bend, the stairwell leading up to the royal quarters came into view across a grand ballroom. I was excited—eager to see where I would spend my nights. Anything was better than the small, lumpy bed in the shared cottage on the isle.

Thana surprised me by not chastising me for my outburst with the captain, but if the wringing of her hands was any indication, she was only waiting until we were alone to reign the fury of the gods down on me.

Laughter echoed from another corridor to our right, the sound growing closer. Perhaps it was my imagination, but Alaric seemed to tense. Two males emerged from the corridor, spilling into the ballroom. I blinked, realizing I had stopped in my slow walk to stare.

They were identical, from their rich honey brown hair to

their laughing ochre eyes. Both shirtless. My fists clenched at my sides. *Why were they shirtless?* Their tan skin shone in the orange glow of sunset filtering in from the arched windows, contouring each of their muscles with strokes of shadow and light. Even their faces were the same, one a perfect mirror image of the other.

The instant they caught sight of Alaric, they raced over, their wings tucked in close to their backs. *Wings!* I had heard of the Draconian race of the Night Court, but they were so rare. Thana told me there was only a handful left.

Once, they could shift their bodies entirely, becoming the dragons of a time long since past. Now, their descendants muddled bloodlines could still produce the leathery black wings and were said to have skin as tough as scales, but nothing more.

"Alaric!" they shouted in unison, rushing to wrap their arms around him—clap him on the back.

"How have things been?" one asksed.

"Camp isn't the same without you. Those useless—"

The one on the right who had been speaking shut his mouth when he noticed Thana and I. The other one followed suit, and in unison, they both dropped to one knee.

"Forgive us, Your Majesty."

Alaric cleared this throat, gesturing to the two males before us, "Your Majesty, this is Kade," he said, pointing to the one on my right, "And Finn," he continued, pointing to the one on the left, "They are—er—*were* in my unit at the Horde camp."

The one called Kade peeked up at Alaric, "And now we're stuck with general whatshisname."

Alaric didn't conceal his laugh, or the shake of his head as he said, "Apologies, majesty. These two are trouble-makers through and through. They do not understand how to act in the presence of royalty."

Kade waggled his thick brows at Alaric, "We were once a trio of trouble-makers if I remember correctly."

Finn punched his brother's arm and together they stood.

"A pleasure to meet you both. And I'm sorry for stealing away your general. He's been very... helpful these past few days."

Kade and Finn shared a look, and I realized what they thought I was implying. And the way they stared at me, brows furrowed as they took in the full length of me, ochre eyes mischievous and glinting with something akin to hunger. My stomach flipped, and a blush crept onto my face before I could turn away.

"The queen needs to rest," Thana scorned, taking my arm in hers, "She has had a very long journey."

Finn brushed a hand through his tousled hair, "Of course. We look forward to seeing you again, and welcome back at court, Your Majesty."

Kade nodded his goodbye, bending into another small bow and they left us. Alaric watched as they walked away, shaking his head as they passed out of view and their laughter began again.

THE ROYAL QUARTERS were not what I was expecting. The rooms themselves were grand. The parlor was large enough to fit the cottage where I grew up threefold, and the bathing room was gigantic, the black marble basin big enough to bathe three people at the same time. And the bed—*the bed!* It was *large* and covered with down pillows and duvets. A quick stroke of the sheets and I knew they were of the finest silk. But everything was white, blank... boring. The furniture was white. The bedding, white. The walls and curtains and carpets, all white.

"You should rest," Thana said, drawing back the covers on the bed.

Despite my protests that Alaric could enter my quarters,

Thana demanded that it would be improper and forced him to stand guard at the entrance.

I wandered out onto the terrace, ignoring her gentle command, taking in the night as it swept over the bay on a warm breeze. Thana came to stand beside me, sighing. "You should be more careful," she said, pushing a stray lock of her auburn hair back from her thin face. "The captain has held his position for many years and holds a good amount of sway with the council. You shouldn't torment him so."

I suppressed the urge to roll my eyes at her, "You are the one who told me to act the part. To not show any weakness. I don't trust him. Why banish all his sentries before I could arrive? That decision should have been mine to make, or at least, to weigh in on."

She placed a light hand on my shoulder, "It was to protect you from harm. If he thought they posed a threat, I'm grateful he was quick to pass judgment, and you should be too. If those sentries had been working with the Day Court to carry out Enya's assassination, they are traitors and could very well have been aiming to end your line."

Then she wouldn't like what I planned to do at the council meeting.

"I don't believe the Day Court is responsible," I told her.

"Then what do you believe?"

I shrugged, sighing, "I don't know."

She huffed, spinning on her heel, her tone threaded with exhaustion as she said, "I'll assemble the council. Get some rest, Liana."

CHAPTER FOUR

*E*ntering the council chambers was like walking into a dragon's den, except, in this case, *I* was the dragon. And I would not allow them to make me feel as though it were the other way around. Thana insisted that she stay behind, explaining that a handmaiden couldn't enter the chamber anyhow and that she would like to retire to her adjoining chambers.

If the only reason had been that she wasn't allowed to enter, I would have told her that was nonsense and she would enter the chamber with me. But I could see the weariness in her eyes and would never force her to do anything.

Alaric moved to stand outside the doorway, but I ushered him inside with us. "I'll need you to come inside with me," I whispered to him and his brows furrowed.

"He may not enter the chamber, majesty," the captain said, drawing unnecessary attention to my arrival. The rest of the council stood in my honor. There were nine people seated at the long oval table, with the captain seated on the left among some of the oldest nobles in the Night Court. To the right sat a male who could only be Silas, the leader of the Horde armies, and a couple of other nobles as well as the court's baron of finance. But it was the male at the head of the table who drew the most attention.

Adorned in a cloak of dark furs, offsetting his silvery hair and deep blue eyes, stood Edris, my father, smiling at me. "Welcome home, Your Majesty," he said, and seemed to mean it.

My teeth clenched against the sentiment in his voice. Not trusting myself to speak to him right away, I turned my gaze instead toward the captain, "Alaric will be joining us for this meeting."

The captain clamped his mouth shut and fell back into his seat, the rest of the council returning to their seats as well. After several minutes of forced formalities and introductions, Edris was the one to break the tension, "I think we'd all agree—we're glad to have you back and for you to take your rightful place at court, but may I ask if there's a reason for this meeting beyond formality?"

"Indeed," the captain intoned, "All seems a little rushed. We didn't expect to bring the council together until after your Blessing Ceremony."

With an inward sigh, I clasped my hands together beneath the table, "There is another reason. I would like to make changes regarding the Royal Guard."

After a painful silence, Edris had the decency to be the only one not to be taken aback, "What changes?" he asked simply, a note of curiosity in his tone.

"Effective immediately, I am relieving Ronan of his duties as captain. The council may decide where he would be most needed."

A flurry of whispers broke out in the council chamber. Shock. Dismay. The emotions were plain on their faces. I noticed how Edris remained silent, meeting my eyes with an emotion more like pride. Alaric was a statue at my side, unflinching, the only indication he'd even heard what I said was the slight clenching of his jaw.

"Ridiculous!" Ronan bellowed, moving to stand. "I've held this position for decades."

I stood, and the room quieted.

"Sit down, Ronan," Edris said, crossing his arms over his chest. "Please, go on," he continued, waving his arm in a sweeping arc across the table, looking far too amused by the whole situation.

My skin prickled at the tension in the room. Thana would say I was born for this role. *You're bossy as the gods,* she would often tell me, *and stubborn as a wild stallion.* And my least favorite, *you'll make a fearsome queen someday.* What she never said, but I'm sure she knew, is that though I hated being told what to do, what I hated even more was being the center of attention. It made my skin itch and my heart race.

I supposed now that I'd become queen, I'd have to get over that.

"Ronan will retain his place on the council," I told them, trying to meet each set of eyes, "At least, for now," I amended.

A red-faced Ronan spoke through clenched teeth, "And who will you appoint as captain of your Royal Guard? I *hand selected* those sentries—well aside from Alaric, and they won't follow just anyone, I—"

"And I wouldn't expect them to, which is why the three sentries you *selected* will also be released from their duties as Royal Guardians." *Breathe in, breathe out, pray this isn't a mistake,* "As to your first question, Alaric will assume the title of Captain of the Queen's Guard."

More whispers erupted in the chamber, their volume rising until they seemed to fill the space with hot air, rebounding back from the vaulted ceiling in echoes.

Alaric fell to one knee before me, bowing his head, but not before I could note how his face drained of color, "Your Majesty, I am honored, but—"

"Will you accept the position?"

He brought his head up to search my face, and I forced myself to maintain composure. I wouldn't force him to accept the position, but I hoped he would take it. When the wraiths made an attempt on my life, it was him who dove in to save me. When I was ill, it was him who aided me. And as we walked from the ship, it was him who was at my side, hand on the hilt of his sword, ready for an attack at any moment. I trusted him more than I trusted anyone else in these palace walls, aside from Thana, but Thana didn't train in the Horde, and I doubted she could wield a blade.

He nodded once, sharp, "If it will please you, majesty, I accept. I vow to protect you until my dying breath."

My breathing hitched at the sincerity in his voice, in the stillness of his gaze, "You have free reign to select the sentries who will serve as members of the Royal Guard at your side. I'll give you two moons to choose who they'll be."

Silas, the leader of the Horde armies, stood, "Though I cannot speak to your reasoning for dismissing former Captain Ronan, I can speak to your choice of captain. Even at the top of the chain of command, I was made aware of Alaric's bravery and skill in combat. He served as a respected leader of his regiment. It was I who nominated him as the fourth sentry to join the Royal Guard, and for good reason," and then to Alaric, "Congratulations on your new position."

Alaric nodded, "Thank you, general."

Edris clapped his hands together, all too eager to have the meeting over with, he asked, "Now that that's settled, is there anything else?"

I resumed my seat, signaling to the shifting and fidgeting

dignitaries in attendance I was far from finished, "One last thing. I would like to invite an emissary from the Day Court to my Blessing Ceremony."

CHAPTER FIVE

$\mathcal{C}$haos erupted in the chamber after that. Not a single council member supported my decision. I took each of their concerns into consideration, but none of them could change my mind. The *feud* with the Day Court was unjustified. There was no proof they were to blame for the fall of Enya.

When I asked the council why there were no open lines of communication between courts, they said it was because the Fae of the Day Court lived like savages. They fought to the death for entertainment and took more than one mate. The denizens of the Day Court danced naked under the moon and drank to the sun. They were devious and not to be trusted. Maybe that way of life *was* strange—foreign. But to them, our way of life could seem just as strange.

Then there was the presentation of other matters that needed attention, like invitations to the Solstice Ball, and a disturbance in a northern village that ended with the disappearance of two Fae nobles, a male, and a female. It was all so trivial, and if I was being honest, a total bore. I didn't care who came to the ball or didn't, and it was obvious the two nobles had simply run off together, considering their homes were empty.

"You did what?" Thana asked, aghast when I returned to my chambers to find her awake and explained what I'd done.

"I didn't trust Ronan, so, I fixed it. And I want to know more about the Day Court, and why everyone thinks they're at fault for Enya's assassination, so, I found a way to learn more," I shook my head in exasperation. It had been a long night and soon, the sun would rise. I couldn't handle another interrogation, "Isn't that what you told me to do? Surround myself with people I trust? To learn quickly? And to trust my own judgment?"

"Well, yes, but—"

"Please, Thana, tell me you support my decision." I needed at least one person to understand. I wasn't raised at court. I didn't have the same prejudices as the others or the same way of thinking. I knew no one. I was all alone in the palace save for Thana, and I needed her on my side.

She took a long, exaggerated breath, "I support you, Liana. I always will." She came forward to wrap me in a hug, "Even if I think you've lost your mind."

I laughed against her shoulder, "Thank you."

"Now," she exhaled, pulling away, "On a less somber note, there's a tailor waiting in the parlor to take your measurements."

I scrunched my eyebrows, "What for?"

A slight roll of her eyes told me I should already know, but my mind was foggy and filled with longing for my bed, "For your gown." She threw her arms up when I still didn't understand what she was on about, "For your *Blessing Ceremony*. It's in two days, Liana, or had you forgotten?"

"Oh."

"Oh?'" She took my arm to pull me towards the parlor, "Honestly, Liana, it's one of the most important days of your life, how could you forget?"

And she was right, it was an important day. And I had

forgotten. In two days my ancestors would decide which of the Graces to bestow me with—if they Graced me with anything at all. *They have to,* I thought, because, without a Grace, I could never keep my throne.

"Ah, there she is!" a short male squealed as we entered the parlor, rising from his seat on one of the oversized settees. "Such beauty!" he exclaimed, taking my hand in his and twirling me around. I was so taken aback that I nearly fell on my face when he released me. The male bent to one knee in an exaggerated bow and righted his ornate green and gold tunic, which matched the coloring of his squinty eyes, "My name is Darius, majesty, and I'm honored to be your tailor," and then to Thana, "Lovely to see you again, my darling, it's been some time."

"Darius," Thana said by way of greeting with a nod.

"A pleasure to meet you, Darius. Thank you for coming on what I'm sure was very short notice."

The tailor wasped the thought away with a flick of his hand, "I heard you were with the council almost the whole night through, so we'll make fast work of this."

"Word travels fast."

Darius helped me to stand atop a small pedestal, pulling several things from a leather case near my feet, "Oh yes, majesty. Nosey bunch here at court, be careful who your trust, and who you confide in."

"I shall," I told him, helping him remove my skirts and corset to get a better measurement.

A small sound drew my attention to the doorway, and I turned to find Alaric there, staring at my all but bare backside, a slight blush crawling its way up his neck. Of course, he would need to be present when someone entered by chambers. For safety. And I had to admit, I enjoyed the way he watched me, with something like admiration painting his otherwise stoic features.

"Alaric, have you chosen your sentries for my Royal Guard?"

He cleared his throat, "Yes, majesty. I've sent riders to notify them. They should arrive by this evening for your approval."

"Good. You can station them to guard the royal chambers and retire to the captain's quarters this evening when they arrive, Ronan's things should be removed by then. You need your rest, captain."

He nodded.

The tailor scribbled several numbers down in a leather-bound journal before rising, hands on his hips, "Now, the traditional style of gown for a Blessing Ceremony is white—very conservative," he said with a tight-lipped smile, "But are there any particular fabrics or embellishments you'd like added?"

I thought about it for a moment, taking in the ghastly white room around me, imagining the same dull shade draped around me, cloying at my neckline, and all the way down to my wrists. *Ugh.* "I won't wear a white gown. Or anything too constricting. I'll let you decide the color and the style."

"Liana, the noble families will think it an insult to tradition if you wear anything but white," Thana tsked from her perch on the arm of the settee.

I gave her a mischievous grin, earning myself one of her exasperated sighs, then I told her, "You of all people should know, I'm *not* traditional."

It could have been my imagination, but I could have sworn I heard Alaric chuckle.

"Praise the gods! A queen with a mind of her own. It will be my pleasure to craft for you a gown that breaks tradition."

CHAPTER SIX

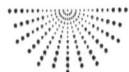

The official farewell to the fallen queen took place before we arrived. Alaric wasn't exaggerating when he told me how covered her tomb was in offerings. Deep below the palace, in the cavernous catacombs lay my mother, in a coffin of polished gray stone. Hundreds of softly flickering candles surrounded the raised platform, along with thousands of white flowers—each enchanted by the those Graced in earth and fire, so the candles would never burn out, and the flowers, never wilt.

My being there was a formality. They expected for me to grieve her loss, and to lay an offering of my own on her tomb. When Thana asked me if she should summon a Graced noble to enchant my offering, I told her it wasn't necessary.

The air in the catacombs was cold and thick with moisture and the unpleasant odor of mold. Alaric unclasped his cloak and draped it over my shoulders, "Are you alright, majesty?" he asked, true concern flitting into and out of his gaze.

"Yes. Fine." I told him. He likely thought it was sadness that made my jaw clench and my hands ball into fists. *Good, let him think that.* Because the truth was ugly. I hated her. I was angry. Upset she never gave me the chance to know her.

She left me to rot on that island my entire mortal life, never once coming to see me, or even sending a letter. All for my *protection.* All because once, a very long time ago, her first-born child was taken from her, found dead beyond the line separating the Night Court from the Wastes. Perhaps it was that she couldn't stand the sight of me, only bearing me so that her line could someday continue. Either way, she was no mother of mine.

With barely concealed restraint, I pulled my offering from the concealed pocket of my gown and placed it at the center of her tomb.

Thana gasped. Alaric stiffened. I knew what they would think, but I didn't care. It was customary to leave flowers, or a candle, for someone you mourned—someone you would miss. But I would do neither of those things.

The ashen gray pebble looked out of place among the flowers and flames. I chose one small enough to carry, but not so small it wouldn't be noticed, from the shore where I spent my childhood skipping stones. It was her death that set me free, and now, it was her turn to be trapped in stone.

THAT EVENING, Thana retired to her chamber early, saying she had enough excitement for one day. For me, the thought of sleep flitted away sometime ago, my body and mind wired from days spent with so much, well, everything. So many people. So many sights, sounds, smells. I was high on the effect of it all.

Alaric stood guard as the servants laid the table with more food than I'd ever seen in my life, only relaxing his strained posture after the royal taster, a pretty female whose name I'd already forgotten tasted each of the dishes.

"Join me," I asked more than ordered him as the servants left. "There's enough here to feed the entire Horde."

He pulled a chair from against the wall and set it to my right, "Yes, majesty."

"Liana," I corrected him, "There's no one else here, we can drop the formalities."

He relaxed into the chair, "Forgive me for saying this Liana, but you're unlike any female I've ever met. And certainly not what I was expecting."

I filled my plate with roast meats and some sort of fruit that was the richest color of red I'd ever seen, smirking, I asked him, "And what *did* you expect?"

Alaric filled his own plate with a monstrous helping from each platter, smiled, "I don't know, maybe for you to be more..."

"More queenly?"

He chuckled, and I stopped mid chew to admire the dimples in his cheeks. He was a *fine* male. I couldn't find a single flaw in his face. "Yes, that. Exactly that."

"Sorry to disappoint you," I teased, pouring both myself and him wine from an ivory pitcher.

I was about to ask him if he'd heard anything about the Day Court emissary's arrival. The Queen of the Day Court had not only accepted the invitation, but hand selected someone to attend my Blessing Ceremony—when a servant entered the room, unable to hide her surprise at finding Alaric seated at my table, "Your sentries have arrived, captain. Should I tell them to wait outside?"

Alaric moved to stand, but it was me who answered, "Send them in."

The servant bowed and left the room. Alaric busied himself brushing crumbs from his leather armor, his lips firmly sealed.

I heard them before I saw them and knew straight away who he'd selected. Pushing myself from the table, I stood to greet the winged twins as they barged into the room.

"Hello again," I said, pushing my hair back behind my shoulders.

Alaric came to stand at my side, leaning in close to my ear, "I know I said they were trouble-makers, but they're loyal, and two of the best fighters I commanded. I can... choose others if you'd like."

"Trying to get rid of us already?" one drawled, a brow raised. He took my hand, planting a warm kiss on the back. "Your Majesty, we'll protect you with our lives."

"We are at your service," the other added, his tone serious and voice deep. I shivered. Protection was great and all, but what about other kinds of service... *Stop it, Liana!*

Alaric pulled my hand from the twin who still held it, "Enough, you two. She still hasn't appro—"

"I approve." I couldn't help it, I was *beaming* at them.

"The council has petitioned to select the other two sentries," Alaric said, "But, of course, you will have the final say."

I nodded, unable to wipe the smile from my face. Kade was the one who had kissed my hand, and Finn was the other. I could find nothing to physically to tell them apart—but where Finn was calm and cool, with a pensive stare and steady eyes, Kade was the opposite. He had an aloofness, and a crooked mischievous smile that made me want to break all the rules.

They were known as trouble-makers, and I bet they knew how to have fun. I was looking forward to knowing what that would be like.

Maybe they can teach me.

I turned back to the table, pouring two more chalices with wine, "A toast," I announced, "To the Captain of the Royal Guard and his sentries."

The twins needed no coercion and took the chalices from my outstretched hands.

"And to Liana, the Queen of the Night Court," Alaric said,

lifting his own chalice from the table and handing me mine, "Long may she reign."

"Long may she reign," Kade and Finn echoed.

I tipped the contents of my chalice back, savoring the tart sweetness as it slid down my throat and warmed my insides. I knew that flavor, even concealed as it was in the wine.

"No!" I shouted, lunging to knock the chalice from Alaric's hand, it's contents pitching onto the white rug. "Stop, don't drink it!" I shouted again before either of the twins could do more than wet their lips. "Spit it out," I ordered.

"Your Majesty?" Alaric's eyes widened, and his face drained of color, "What is it?"

The pain began in my stomach, reaching its burning claws up the back of my neck, causing a thunderous ache in my head. I swayed. Kade caught me, his strong arms curling around my shoulders. Finn and Alaric raced to my side. "Verbane," I choked out.

"Finn, go get a healer, now!" Finn charged to the balcony as opposed to the door and I watched as he spread his great black wings. They were magnificent, strong, and unlike anything I'd ever beheld.

"Wait," I called to him, earning myself confused looks from the threesome. The pain already subsiding to a tolerable level, I told them, using Kade as a crutch to get back to my feet, "It won't kill me. It's just... uncomfortable."

"But, Liana, the poison—"

I shook my head, "I've been eating verbane berries since I was a child. I'm all but immune to its effect."

The three of them shared a look, Finn not moving from his place at the balcony's edge.

"That is incredibly smart, majesty," Kade said, leaning in, one arm still braced at the small of my back. His breath caressed my neck, raising the small hairs there. He smelled of spice and something akin to the forest on a hot day. Intoxicating.

I could have told them it wasn't purposely done, that I was a stubborn child who liked the tart sweetness and nothing more, but I kept my mouth shut instead. Let them think I was smart and cunning, perhaps one day, I would be.

Alaric blew out a strained breath, the color returning to his face, "Indeed," he agreed with Kade, "But we should send for the healer anyway, if only to ease your discomfort."

"No," I stated, "I will not give the person to blame for this the satisfaction of knowing they succeeded."

Finn nodded his agreement, striding to where I now stood, legs still not steady enough to stand on my own, "She's right," he said, "The walls of this palace have eyes and ears. The denizens of the Night Court shouldn't know what happened here."

"The taster," Kade said, his hand now rubbing soothing circles into my back, setting my nerve-endings ablaze, "We should—"

Alaric lifted me into his arms, taking me from a jealous looking Kade. I wrapped my arms around his neck, relishing in his musky vanilla scent. He strode from the room, his face set in stone.

Before we entered my chamber, he called back, "Find the taster. If she isn't dead, follow her. She could lead us to the person responsible."

CHAPTER SEVEN

$\mathcal{I}$ didn't tell Thana what happened the night before. She would only be sick with worry. I let her putter about my chamber, commenting on the late morning hour and how I *had* to get out of bed. There were things to do, apparently. My Blessing Ceremony was the following day, and I had yet to decide what I would like for the feast that followed.

"The cooks need notice for these things, you know. They can't conjure food from thin air."

Alaric bit back a laugh, causing Thana to tremble with frustration, "And what did I tell you," she chastised, "*He* should not be allowed to enter your bedchamber, it's—it's..."

"Improper?" I finished for her, with a quirk of my brow.

Thana shook her head.

Alaric hadn't left my chamber since the night before, standing diligent guard over me while I slept off the poison still setting my veins ablaze. It had been strong. The verbane must've been distilled to increase its potency. I was only sick once in the night, and Alaric was there, holding my hair as I wretched into the ornate basin. Though I felt as though I'd spent the eve drinking Thana's store of wine as I had when I was still mortal,

I was trying to maintain a façade of strength. If only to ease the lines of worry still carved around his eyes.

"Improper," Thana mimicked, "Indeed!"

I threw back the covers, hauling myself from their warm embrace, "Then you'll speak of it to no one, will you?"

She huffed, tossing me a robe that I took my time wrapping around myself, "And raise even *more* questions from the nobles than you already have? I think not."

"Good."

Thana tossed a simple lilac gown into my arms, turning to leave the room, "Dress yourself," she said with a hint of bitterness, "The cooks are waiting for instruction. *I'll* tell them to make what they please since *you* have no opinion on the matter."

Alaric crossed his arms over his broad chest, watching Thana leave the room, "Why do you allow her to speak to you in such a way?"

I hadn't ever considered I had any say in the way she spoke to me. It was how she *was*, and I had grown accustomed to her temperament, had grown to love her more for it. Thana would always say what she meant, without worry about the repercussions. In that way, she was of great value—even if she could be the most vexing creature I'd known—I wouldn't change a thing about her. She was the closest thing to a mother I would ever know.

"If you knew what I put her through as a child, you'd be more surprised she didn't simply drown me and be done with it."

His lips twitched up into a half-smile, "How are you feeling?" he asked, changing the subject as I stepped behind the privacy screen to change.

"Better," I told him, stripping off my robe and night clothes to step into the gown, "Thank you… for staying with me."

Not that I was afraid, though I had considered the possibly that once the culprit found out I still lived, they'd try to finish me off in my sleep, no—it was nice to have someone there, to not be alone.

I heard him clear his throat before he spoke, "It's my duty to ensure your safety, Liana. I would have stayed even if you'd ordered me to go."

He must've known what he was saying was imprudent, and that disobeying a direct order from his queen could warrant serious consequences, but my heart leapt at his words—affirming my choice to make him my captain.

"Could you help me with this?" I stepped from behind the screen, clutching the bodice of the flowing gown to my chest to hold it in place.

I was hopeless with corsets, always had been. The thin strings laced at the back were impossible for my clumsy fingers.

Alaric's eyes traveled the length of the gown, finally stopping to rest on where my hands cupped the fabric around my breasts. A soft growl escaped his lips before he could reign himself in, the reverberations pulled at something deep in my belly.

Without a word, he strode to where I stood, and I turned to plant my hands on the bedpost. His hands wove the strings into place, grazing the soft skin on the small of my back. I had to grit my teeth against the sounds trying to tumble from my lips as he pulled the strings tight. It wasn't pain or discomfort, but some other thing I couldn't name.

"There," he said, planting his hands on either side of my waist, spinning me around, "I hope I did that right."

So, so right. I reveled in the tender touch of his hands, warm where they still held my waist.

KADE RETURNED hours later with no news other than to tell us the taste—who's name was Selbi, was alive but hadn't led them anywhere helpful. Finn was still following her around, "When I left, the taster was in the kitchens, and before that she was in her chambers, asleep."

"And there's no possibility she left her bed?"

Kade's eyes widened as though Alaric had asked him the most condescending question, "No. I stayed close to her door, and Finn kept watch over her window from outside. She never left."

Alaric's eyebrows furrowed. "Well we can't have her tasting Liana's food—"

"Liana?" Kade asked, a cheeky grin pulling at the corners of his mouth.

"Yes, Liana. That is my name, the last I checked," I drawled, rising from the settee in the parlor.

"Why do you get to call her by her name?" Kade asked in a whisper he likely thought I couldn't hear, his words laced with jealousy and suspicion.

"You may call me by my name as well," I offered, and his face split into a magnificent grin, "Now, will you two stop talking about me as if I'm not here? The taster will continue to taste my meals until we've learned something useful from her. If we replace her, she'll be suspicious," I held up a hand when Alaric tried to inject a rebuttal, "If you'd like, you can have a second taster come in after her, but Selbi is not to know of the second taster's presence."

Kade, still grinning from learning he could call me by name, agreed, "She has a point."

"Fine. Find someone discreet to be the second taster, and then take shifts tracking Selbi," Alaric retorted, rubbing his eyes. He was likely exhausted, as far as I knew, he hadn't slept since we disembarked from the ship.

I shook my head, "No, Kade will stay with me," I told him, gesturing to the winged male, "You need to rest."

He didn't disagree, nodding, "Very well."

Kade couldn't conceal his excitement, it poured from him in

waves of heat that made me take a step back. Fire. That must be his Grace. I wondered if his brother was Graced the same.

Alaric whispered something to Kade before shooting me a meaningful look and lumbering out of the room. Kade watched his captain leave before turning to me, rubbing his enormous hands together, "So, *Liana,* where do you want me?"

NOT MORE THAN AN HOUR LATER, Kade and I were walking the halls of the palace. I wanted to see the Great Hall where I would be the star-attraction at the ceremony tomorrow. I need to know what I was walking into, you know, so I didn't trip, or otherwise make a complete fool of myself. Kade had been blessed, he could tell me what I was meant to do since Thana hadn't yet returned from the kitchens.

"You have nothing to be worried about," Kade drawled, focused and yet flippant at the same time, "It's all a formality, really. You walk up to the cauldron, fill the ewer and pour yourself a drink—then you drink it. You'll get a taste of your Grace, everyone will cheer. Then we feast. The end."

He had no idea it wasn't being able to pour my own drink that worried me, but about what I would be Graced with. Would it be fire, the most difficult Grace to control, or would it be something useless, like the ability to understand animals or commune with spirits? Or, the most terrifying—to not be Graced at all. It had happened to many Fae who went to drink the water of the Sidhe, but never to a queen, or even a noble.

But there's a first time for everything.

"Easy," I agreed, trying to maintain an air of confidence.

We rounded a bend in the corridor and the Great Hall materialized before us. It was quite the room, and I had to work to lift my jaw from where it'd fallen to my feet.

The parquet floor was polished to perfection, midnight black, and starlight gray tile patterned for one hundred paces. A maroon carpet cleaved the room in two, running straight up the middle, over the few stairs, and onto the dais. There, the golden cauldron waited, wisps of bluish fog dancing along the surface of the water. The ceiling was arched, and ornately designed with a mixture of tile and beam. Six chandeliers hung in pairs down its length.

Servants milled about, some cleaning, and others arranging flowers.

Suddenly, I didn't want to wait any longer. I wanted to get the damned ceremony finished with. But it was one tradition I would uphold. They expected it of me, of *any* noble to complete the proper ceremony in order to be Graced. But it was so frustrating. *Why do they all need to watch?*

"Do you want to get closer?" Kade asked me, gesturing to the cauldron.

I scowled, "No—I don't."

He quirked a brow at me, his flippancy replaced by something more like worry.

"What do you do around here for fun?"

Kade crossed his arms over his broad chest, considering. "I'm not supposed to let you leave the palace grounds."

My eyebrows furrowed, "Says who?"

"Alaric."

"Well then consider his request refused."

His answering grin was infectious, and I yelped when he grabbed my hand and took off in a full sprint from the room, dragging me along with him.

We stopped at a small balcony, and he climbed onto the ledge, "Are you afraid of heights?" he asked, a challenge in his stare as he unfurled his wings.

My heart plummeted into my stomach, but not in fear—or at least, I didn't think so. No, it was elation. I didn't have time to respond before he pulled me up, wrapping his arms around my middle.

And then we fell.

I shrieked at the rushing of the wind. It was exhilarating, terrifying—pure bliss. When he flipped around, his wings caught the air current and we sprang upwards. I laughed, my eyes wet with unshed tears from the force of the wind.

Fun. I was having *fun*.

I was still laughing when he pushed us ever higher, gliding on the air currents until we were hovering over the bay, almost in reach of the clouds. I shivered against the chill of the oncoming night, and he held me tighter in response, his body heating with his Grace of fire. I shivered again.

"Don't worry, I won't drop you," he told me, with a mischievous leer that made me think he just might.

"This is incredible," I said between fits of giggles. The sun had sunk low, setting the sky ablaze with an orange and rose glow. Far below us, the palace was awash in the colors, and the water in the bay reflected them back at us. At that height, I could see the Wastes clearly, a maze of trails through the ashy mountain range. And far in the distance, if I squinted, I thought I could just make out the original palace of the Night Court— now nothing more than a ruin blending almost seamlessly into the rock face of Mount Noctis.

"Alaric would kill me if he knew I had you out here."

"Our secret?" I asked him, tilting my head up so I could meet his ochre stare. He really was magnificent—chiseled features shadowed by honeyed bronze facial hair and deep-set eyes. In the light of the setting sun, he could have been a painting of some long-forgotten king. I reached over his shoulder to stroke his right wing, and his entire body tensed in response. It was like satin, but with the strength and hardness of something more solid. They shimmered when he moved them as though a million specks of diamond were embedded within.

Kade winked at me, "Yeah, our secret."

Something caught his eye from below and I turned in his

arms to find what drew him. There, on the southern road leading to the palace, was a lone rider on horseback. Kade swooped lower, causing my stomach to drop again, until we were close by the palace, but concealed in a copse of trees.

The horse was a white stallion, and if the panting of the animal was any indication, it had carried its rider far. The rider was... odd. He was dressed in shades of topaz with a belt and reigns of gold. His hair was also golden, and longer than most males, reaching to his shoulders.

A falcon flew over the male in wide circles, never letting the rider out of his sight.

Kade grew hot at the sight of the foreign rider, scalding my back and legs where his bare arms held me. He kept the malice it was obvious he felt out of his voice as he gave me a wan smile that didn't reach his eyes, "Your emissary has arrived."

CHAPTER EIGHT

*T*he servants came in after Kade and I returned, him lowering me gently onto the balcony of my bedchamber. Luckily, no one saw us arrive, though they seemed surprised to find us in the royal quarters. Thana, it seemed, had been looking for me.

They told me the Day Court emissary had arrived, and was escorted to the opposite tower, He was given the quarters meant for noble guests, as I had instructed. I told the servants I would not formally receive him that night, blaming the late hour and the need to rest before my Blessing Ceremony tomorrow afternoon. The truth was that I was nervous. I had no idea what he would be like—or if the council was right about them, if he would try to kill me outright.

No, I would receive him tomorrow, just before the ceremony, with more than one armed sentry at my side.

Kade and I sat at the table in the dining room, laughing about something Finn had said to him earlier when Thana burst in.

"Where have you been?" she asked, hands on her hips.

I subdued my laughter long enough to reply, "Kade took me

on a tour of the palace," I told her, failing to mention that part of the tour was held in the sky.

"And why did no one know where—"

Alaric paused in the doorway, a frightened boy in tow behind him. "A tour of the palace?" he directed his question towards Kade, who only shrugged in response. "You remained on the palace grounds, as I requested?"

Kade faltered, "Well, I—"

"We did." I answered for him. "The brute wouldn't let me leave the front gates."

He looked much better than that morning. Some color had returned to his face, and his silvery blue eyes seemed brighter, more alert. He corralled the boy forward to the table, and it was then I noticed the manacles on his hands and feet, clanking as he walked.

"What is this?" I asked Alaric, teeth clenched as I beheld the boy. It was plain to see he had not yet transitioned from mortal to Fae and couldn't have been more that sixteen. His dull brown hair was matted and greasy—his face streaked with what looked like soot.

Alaric looked just as displeased with the situation as I was and handled the boy gently as he nudged him forward, "This is your second taster. His name is Rin. He's guilty of attempting to take the water of the Sidhe without royal consent. He will remain a prisoner until the council decides his fate."

I understood Alaric's decision, but that didn't mean I had to like it. As a prisoner confined to the dungeons, the boy could tell no one of his position as a taster. So long as someone Alaric trusted guarded him, and escorted him to and from my chamber in secret, no one would know.

"Hello, Rin," I said to him, and he raised his head in response, revealing a handsome face beneath the layers of dirt and eyes the color of wheat. He looked tired, and hungry, and maybe a little frightened, though the tension in his jaw told me he was trying to hide it. "This is a dangerous job, but if you help me, I'll do my best to help you get out of this mess you've got yourself in."

He inclined his head in a bow, "Yes, majesty. I would like that very much."

I nodded to Alaric, gesturing to his shackles. He hesitated for only a moment before relenting to my silent request. The manacles fell to the floor, and the boy rubbed his sore wrists, raw and red from the iron circlets.

"You will speak to no one of what you're doing here," Kade injected.

"I need this to remain between us, and only us. If you do your part, I *will* help you—starting now. Once you're through tasting the dishes," I waved an arm over the table before us, laden with roast meats, fruits, and cheeses, "I'll see you're fed and clothed properly. And a bath, perhaps?"

He nodded fervently, eyes glazed with hunger as he beheld the bounty before him.

"Go ahead," I prodded, handing him a fork and the duller of my two knives. "Small bites and wait a moment between each tasting. You can survive a small amount of poison with the proper care."

"Yes, Your Majesty," he answered, taking his first bite.

I SLEPT RESTLESSLY. Tossing and flopping about the bed until sleep claimed me.

I was dreaming. I had to be. My arms were heavy. Chains. Metal bit into my wrists. I was manacled to a wall in a dungeon somewhere far below the earth—surrounded in cobwebs and slick, cold stone. There was no light, save for what crept in through a small slit beneath a heavy-looking wooden door. I yanked at the manacles, but it was no use. I fumbled around the wall, but there was nothing. No way out.

I screamed, and I screamed, but no one came to rescue me. No one was on the other side of that door, and no one heard me. I was alone. And I was trapped.

"Liana," a voice called, and then louder, "Liana!"

I came back to myself, bolting upright in my bed. It was dark. Sweat covered me in a thin layer of ice, made even cooler by the breeze spilling into the room from the balcony. I shivered, heaving in the chill night air to quell the constriction in my lungs.

"Liana," Alaric said again, calmer, cupping my face between his warm palms. I pushed myself into him and he tensed. His intoxicating vanilla scent enveloped me, and I was almost immediately at peace... and embarrassed. I hadn't had a night terror like that in years, not since I was still mortal.

He wrapped his arms around me, and I leaned into his chest. It was safe. I was safe. The trembling stopped, and I sighed in relief.

"Are you alright?"

I tilted my chin up, "Better," I sighed again, my muscles relaxing.

"Good," he replied, tucking my damped hair behind one ear, "If using my Grace on you makes you uncomfortable, I apologize."

My stomach clenched, "Your Grace?"

Alaric narrowed his gaze at me, cocking his head to one side, "You didn't know? My Grace is touch. I can make anyone feel anything I want them to so long as my skin is in contact with theirs."

"Oh."

He moved his arms out of the way as I moved to sit up. *Touch.* Of course. That thing he did on the ship wasn't an old sailors trick. He made the nausea go away using his Grace. It seemed a useful ability though not as revered as the sort which could be used offensively.

I lifted one of his hands from the bed, clasping it in my own. "Do it again."

He lifted a brow, "Are you sure?"

"Make me feel… confident."

"Confident?"

I dropped his hand, "Yes, confident."

He shook his head, but lifted my hand back into his again, "You're a queen, and you seem fairly confident already."

The sensation rushed over me in a wave, electrifying my body in the most amazing way. My back arched, and my head cleared. I considered the room through a new set of eyes, knowing what had to be done. "I hate all this white. Everything is *so* white. Have Thana summon a decorator tomorrow. I don't wish to live in a replica of my mother's chambers."

Alaric laughed, clasping my hand tighter, "Alright, as you wish, anything else?"

I surveyed him, took in the sound of his voice, the eagerness to please written all over his maddeningly handsome face. Holding his gaze, with my free hand I moved his hair from his face—then traced a line down to his jaw, to his collar-bone, and planted my hand on his chest. He shivered, and a hunger awoke inside me. My hand wandered ever lower, and he growled with desire. I wanted to touch him, wanted him to touch me back. Wanted—

Alaric let go of my hand, shoving himself from the bed and leaving me in a daze. I tried to shake my head to clear it of the thoughts still clasping to become reality. *What was I doing?* What would I have done if he hadn't let go?

"Damn, Liana. Have you any idea what you're doing to me?"

My cheeks inflamed, "I—I'm sorry, I don't know what I was doing."

But I did know. Something attracted me to him. And whether he used his Grace on me, he made me feel safe. The confidence boost was meant to make me less nervous about the

Blessing Ceremony, but when I saw him, I—well I almost did something I obviously wanted to do, whether I knew it or not.

"No, I'm sorry," he breathed, sitting back down on the bed beside me, "I shouldn't have done that."

"It's not your fault. I *wanted* to do tha—I mean," I corrected, "I asked you to do it."

He hung his head, "Liana, you're a queen. And I'm meant to protect you, nothing more. That is how it should be."

A mix of shame and guilt swirled through me, making the blush return to my cheeks. "May I ask why you aren't bonded?"

It was deathly still and quiet for an age before he responded, "I've never been... interested. Bonding yourself to someone— the ceremony, it would tie you to that person forever. They can't undo it, and the link that comes with it cannot be severed."

He regarded me then, his eyes filled with sadness and some-thing like longing, "I haven't met someone who could make me want to become one with them. I doubt I ever will."

I understood what he meant. Though I often fantasized about the day I would be forever bonded to a male of my choos-ing, it wasn't customary for a queen to do, and I wasn't certain I wanted to anyway. The queen's in our line chose a male to reproduce with, and declared them 'King Consort,' they had virtually no power and could only rule in interim periods between the fall of one queen and the bestowal of the crown on another.

I had yet to wear my crown—hadn't even seen it yet. Seemed pompous to wear it around everywhere. But for an event like the Blessing Ceremony, they would expect it. *Ugh.* It was like a beacon saying *over here, look at me! In case you didn't know, I'm the queen. See this crown? Yes, you must do as I say.* Ridiculous.

The tension returned to my muscles all at once and I began my decent down the rabbit-hole of insecurity and over-thinking again. Sleep would be impossible, and there were still hours until dawn would break.

Alaric stood, "I should let you get back to sleep. It's nearly morning and you'll need your strength when the Sidhe bestow a Grace on you, the flare of power takes its toll."

I grabbed him by the hand before he could move away, unsure of what I was doing—what I wanted. Perhaps the feigned confidence was still running through my veins... But before I could change my mind, "Will you stay with me?"

His eyes softened, "I'll be right over there," he whispered, pointing to the place where he usually stands in the corner of the room.

Riling up what was left of my courage, I amended, "No, I mean stay here... in the bed. And keep me calm so I can sleep?"

"I don't think—"

"Please?"

Tight-lipped, Alaric nodded, and removed the boots from his feet. "Move over," he said, more playfully than with any true malice.

He positioned himself in the center of the bed, on top of the down-filled coverlet, and I crawled in next to him. "Here," he said and pulled my upper half onto his chest. I rested my head against him, listening to the steady beating of his heart. My own heart constricted for an instant before he wrapped an arm around me, resting his hand against the skin of my bare arm. I remember nothing but feeling a sense of calm and tranquility before I drifted back to sleep.

CHAPTER NINE

*T*he gown was a work of art. I'd seen nothing even remotely like it. Although I'd be the first to admit I dearly missed the freedom of my trousers and threadbare tunics, there was something to be said about a pretty dress too. Words escaped me, and for the first time, I *saw* what I imagined a queen to look like when I beheld my reflection in the mirror.

The cut was modest without being cloying, giving my curves the perfect hourglass shape. And the fabric, *the fabric*—a deep blue at first glance, but then also purple and pink and silver when I moved, as though Darius cut a swath from the night sky. The bodice was ruched and without true sleeves, but rather small bits of fabric that encircled my upper arms. And the bottom part of the gown was made up of pieces of the same fabric, all in varying lengths and widths—ever-moving, flowing, as if on a phantom breeze.

The way Thana styled my hair was less intricate—and less painful, than any style she had done before. Braided, and pleated. Half of it swooped back, and the rest left to drop gracefully in gentle waves down my back. It was simple, and yet very elegant. The coal she painted on my eyelids did wonders to bring out the deep blue of my irises, and the deep, almost purplish red now staining my lips made them fuller. I seemed older even though I would never age.

All I was missing was the crown—which I sent Thana to retrieve from the royal treasury.

"May I take your silence to mean you like it, majesty?" Darius inquired, standing just off to the side of my reflection in the tall mirror.

Finally, I allowed myself the squeal I'd been holding in to squeeze past my lips, "I love it! It's—It's—"

"Perfect." Finn said, walking into the room from the arched entryway. It was easier to tell them apart now. Finn looked too serious to be confused with his brother, and Kade too much the opposite.

"You look like the Night incarnate," Alaric agreed, "Beautiful."

I stepped from the pedestal and wrapped Darius in a monstrous hug, causing the slight male to wheeze. "Thank you."

Darius patted me on the back, and I released him, glad to see his eyes blazing with pride. Good, he should be proud. He would be my *only* tailor from then on, I had decided.

"You are most welcome."

"Where's Kade?" I asked Finn, stepping down from the raised platform.

A flash of disappointment was clear in the set of his jaw as he cleared his throat to answer, "He's following Selbi. If she doesn't attend the ceremony, then he won't be either."

I doubted Selbi would attend the ceremony, she wasn't of noble birth. But she would be at the feast which meant Kade would be there too, but, "Do we have a plan for the feast?"

It took a moment for Alaric to discern my meaning, and it was Finn who answered, "I doubt there will be—"

Alaric silenced Finn with a cold stare, his gaze resting on

Darius. And as much as I wanted to trust the male, I knew it wasn't wise.

"Shall I go, majesty?" Darius asked, picking up on the energy in the room.

Lifting my skirts, I fell onto the ugly white settee and gave him a small nod, "Can I expect to see you at the ceremony this evening?"

He bowed low, lifting his case as he rose again, "I wouldn't miss it."

"Thank you again," I told him earnestly, running a hand over the satiny smooth fabric covering my lap, "It's incredible. I'd like a room to match it, if that's possible. All this white gives my head pains."

"Poor taste, your late mother, I'm afraid," he sighed, "If you'd like, I'll collaborate with the royal decorator and see what we can come up with."

I rose again to clasp Darius' hand in my own, his were smooth, so much unlike the calloused hands of my sentries I'd become accustomed to, "I would like that."

Without another word, Darius planted a quick kiss on the back of my hand and fled the chamber.

"You should be more careful what you say in front of mixed company," Finn said, his tone clipped.

I motioned for the two males to sit, settling back onto the settee.

"Rin will taste the dishes before they leave the kitchens," Alaric began.

"I'll oversee it to ensure all the dishes, and the wine, are tasted," Finn added.

"Who's Rin?" Thana asked, coming into the parlor with a gaudy crown atop a deep purple velvet pillow. The ornate design shined with diamonds and other precious stones, the crest of the Night Court standing proudly in the front—a full moon made up of luminescent opal, with black diamond wings on either side. "And why is he tasting your food? Have you replaced the royal taster too?"

The three of us went silent before Alaric cleared his throat, "Selbi will be away attending to a family matter," he lied, "Just a precaution in case she doesn't return in time for the ceremony."

Her raised brows, and paltry sigh told me she wouldn't ask any more questions and was likely even more exhausted with court life than I was already. She dropped the pillow into my lap, "Better put that on. The emissary is waiting for you to receive him in the gardens. The ceremony will begin at dusk, so don't dawdle."

CHAPTER TEN

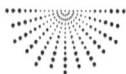

ade and Alaric were tense the entire walk down to the palace gardens. Alaric muttered something about how he should've brought the two sentries the council selected by the royal chambers for my approval. I wondered who they'd selected, and truthfully, didn't want an entourage beyond the three males who had already claimed— and earned, their places by my side.

Besides, the emissary was just one male. What could he possibly do?

The gardens were in full bloom. A provocative scent of blossomed flowers permeated the air long before we entered. The Day Court emissary was seated on a smooth marble bench in the southernmost corner of the garden. He was easy to spot, with his bright colored attire and golden hair. That and the council appointed sentry who hovered a few paces away, watching him like a hawk its prey.

He rose as we drew nearer, exuding confidence, his posture stately and gaze fixed. Once we were close enough to speak, like a fool, I forgot the protocol for welcoming noble guests at court and almost stumbled over a particularly prickly flower bush. The male was unlike any other I had seen at court.

His hair seemed spun of gold and the way it waved accentuated his severe bone structure. High cheekbones framed a lightly tan face and sumptuous lips. His eyes were green, but not easily described. They were the color of a new leaf. The color of the forest after a night of rain. And when he moved his head, this way and that, the color morphed, looking almost yellow in the sunlight.

Finn nudged my side, almost imperceptivity, but it was enough to force words to flow from my lips, "Hello," I stuttered, "I mean, welcome," *Oh crap, I've forgotten his name. Alaric just reminded me...* "I—I hope your journey was a pleasant one."

His lips parted into a half-smile, revealing two rows of perfect teeth, and a dimple in his right cheek.

Suddenly, it was far too hot in the gardens, and I itched to wipe the sweat from the back of my neck, "Your Majesty," he responded, bowing, "My journey was long, but pleasant. It was an honor to receive your invitation. My name is Tiernan, and I offer condolences from the Queen of Day on the passing of your late mother."

He didn't seem like a savage. He seemed, well, very much like the Fae of my court, save for his looks and attire. But looks could be deceiving.

I nodded my thanks, "Please tell me if there is anything I can do to make your stay more comfortable."

"I will," he said, bending to pick a rosebud from the bush at his side, never taking his eyes from me. He stepped forward, causing Alaric and Finn to shift in response, stopping him from moving any closer.

I placed a hand on Alaric's forearm and gave him a pointed stare. His jaw clenched before he jerked his head to Finn and they both took a step back.

Tiernan opened his hand, and I watched in awe as the rose

bud opened, and grew, blossoming into the largest white rose I'd ever seen. He extended his hand and I stepped forward to take pluck it from his palm, twirling it between two fingers.

He inclined his head, "I shall see you this evening, majesty," he said and strolled from the gardens.

MERE MINUTES STOOD between me and the dreaded walk down the maroon carpet to the altar. Alaric, Thana, and Finn would walk behind me, and stand next to me on the dais. Kade was nowhere to be seen.

Thana grasped my trembling hand, and I tried to reign in my nerves. I could hear the chatter from the open alcove where we waited for the sun to set. It was tradition to wait until the sun had fully descended, and the waiting was *killing* me.

Just walk up the aisle. Drink the damned water and walk out. Easy.

"Are you ready?" Thana whispered as the sun dipped below the horizon, bathing the sky in violet light.

I wanted to groan, but the sound came out as more of a sigh, "I am."

I stepped into view of the crowd, standing at the center of the blood-red carpet. The room quieted, stilled, save for a few gasps.

The dress! I had forgotten... A few whispers broke out among the assembly, and I saw more than a few glares of disapproval.

They waited. A throng of nobles and dignitaries—at least one hundred Fae gathered to witness the Blessing of the queen. Servants lined the walls, eyes downcast, waiting with platters of sweet, effervescent wine to serve once the ceremony was complete.

My heart thundered in my chest, scattering my thoughts into oblivion. One step. Two steps. *That's it, Liana, almost there.* By step three, I lost all courage and stopped. But there was

Kade, standing to the side of the altar, an uncharacteristically encouraging countenance on his handsome face. Blowing out a breath, I walked—no, almost jogged to the altar, afraid to lose my nerve again.

There were so many of them watching. Too many. The hairs on the back of my neck and arms raised at the feel of their stares boring into my back—judging me for breaking tradition.

I ascended the stairs and took my place in front of the wide golden cauldron. Thana moved to stand next to Kade, and Alaric and Finn were opposite them, on the other side.

My pulse raced, and I worked to quell the trembling in my fingers.

The water was alive. Below the thin layer of foggy blue was a liquid of indeterminate color. Not blue, as I had assumed, but transparent with shimmers of every color imaginable. It swirled, though no one stirred it, and seemed almost to glow.

The ewer and chalice sat atop a small swooden pedestal to one side. Quickly, I took the ewer and filled it, pouring from the spout into the chalice.

I faltered just before bringing it to my lips. *What if...*

I shook my head and tipped the contents back. It tasted—well it didn't taste like anything at all. But it was cold. And then it was hot. The chill tumbled down into my stomach and then out into each of my veins as though I'd been injected with ice and fire.

With my Fae ears I could hear the assembly collectively take a breath and hold it.

What now?

Alaric, Thana, Finn and Kade watched me. Thana's features swiftly turned to worry. Kade and Finn glanced back and forth at one another. And Alaric's hands balled into fists at his side.

No. *No!* The water didn't work. My ancestors wouldn't Grace me. I would fall to ruin. *I was a disgrace to the crown.* They would overthrow me. An image of myself shackled and in darkness flashed before my eyes. *No...*

The pain began in my chest, and I clutched it, unable to breathe. Alaric was at my side in an instant, holding me up.

It *ached.*

Why did it hurt so much? Was this what it was supposed to feel like?

The agony was all consuming, and I tried—*I tried* to keep calm. Thana's eyes were wide in shock, and Kade and Finn looked horrified. Everything faded into and out of focus. A humming started in my ears, contorting into indeterminable whispers.

I could see the same thought written in the fine print of their stares. Something was wrong. *No, this wasn't supposed to happen.*

My knees collided with the parquet floor, and I grasped the rim of the cauldron to steady myself—it shook. Or was it me who was shaking? Alaric took my face into his hands and gasped when his eyes met mine, letting go as if burned.

The ground splintered below me, and I cried out.

A thundering groan echoed through the Great Hall, met with shouts and the sounds of retreat.

I turned to find the denizens of my court fleeing the room. Flutes of wine shattered in their haste to get out. Only two remained. My father, standing in the middle of the room, his shoulders tense and mouth agape. The other was a blur of turquoise and gold, in the corner of the room, arms crossed over his chest. *Tiernan?*

Spots of color danced in my peripherals and I lurched forward. The pain pulsed and rose, surging and sinking into my bones.

It climaxed in a great and terrible burst. The last thing I heard was an ear-splitting scream before my body buckled under the pressure and I fell into darkness.

CHAPTER ELEVEN

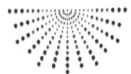

"*I*'ll tell you what I've told you ten times already. She will awaken when she's ready. The queen is strong," a foreign voice said, breaking through the storm clouds in my mind, "It was not poison, I would have felt it. My Grace detects nothing—there is no injury."

"Then why isn't she awake?" Alaric's deep voice bellowed.

"I don't know."

I attempted to move, but my body tensed. And when I opened my eyes a blinding brightness seared them. I sealed them back shut, groaning.

"Too bright," I managed to say and heard Thana gasp from my side.

The mattress moved beneath me, and cool hands caressed my cheeks, "Liana?" she whispered, and I could hear the distress in her words.

Someone dampened the light, and I tried to sit up, steady hands wrapping around my shoulders to help me. Blinking, I cleared my vision enough to see a female I didn't recognize. She removed herself from my bed, Kade, and Finn appearing to take her place. Terror marred Alaric's strong features and darkened his gaze. Somewhere beside me, Thana made a strangled sound.

And Kade, who was about to say something, closed his mouth in stunned silence.

I reached up to touch my face, thinking there must be something there they're staring at. Perhaps I injured myself when I fell? But my fingers traced the curve of my jaw, brushed my hair back and found nothing out of the ordinary.

"What is it?" I asked Thana.

Her lips parted, but she said nothing.

I wasn't Graced. That must be the reason for the fear I saw in their eyes. What would happen to me? Who would reign when the council moved to overthrow me? My father? *Ronan?* The kingdom would fall to ruin under their reign. But... I had no heir to offer. No Grace to secure my crown. I could only imagine the whispers moving through the palace.

Hot tears welled behind my eyelids. My ancestors be damned. I would fight for my place on the throne because that's what queens did. Grace or not, I didn't spend my life preparing, all but alone on the Isle of Mist to give up—to give in. My teeth clenched. "I wasn't Graced, was I?"

Alaric looked away, "It's not that, Liana. We aren't certain whether or not you were Graced. There was no flare of power, but—"

"Then what is it? Why are you all staring at me as though I'm some sort of monster?" No flare of power... That meant no Grace. I was getting angry and wishing they'd all leave.

"Your eyes." Thana said, climbing from the bed to retrieve the small silver mirror from my dressing table.

My reflection looked the same as always, though I'd admit, the skin around my eyes was swollen, and a bit red. "I don't see any—"

Wait... The blue of my irises shifted, the deep shade swirling into a lustrous lilac, and then fading to a metallic silver which darkened to a shade near black. The mirror fell from my hands. My pulse quickened, "What does it mean?"

Finn pursed his lips, "We don't know." And from the set of his jaw and the perturbed look in his eyes, I gathered there wasn't much Finn *didn't* know, and not knowing this tormented him. "I've spent hours going through books and scrolls for two days trying to find out."

Two days? "How long have I been like this?" I struggled to make out the position of the sun in the sky outside the curtained balcony.

"Nearing three days," Alaric answered, and my back stiffened. He took my hand, sending waves of calm through me.

Thana brushed my hair back, running her fingers through the silvery strands like she used to when I was a child. "You'll have to make a formal address to the court."

"Why?"

She sighed, "They're demanding to know what happened... Wondering where you are. A few nobles have petitioned the council to put Edris on the throne."

"He's been trying to enter your chamber since the ceremony, but we didn't know what to tell him," Alaric said, "He wanted to see you were alright."

I balked, "You mean to see if I've been Graced so he knows what his chances are of winning the crown?"

Not one of them disagreed with my statement. Edris was beloved by the denizens of my court. The nobles respected him. But there was something about him—something ingenuine that set my teeth on edge. I didn't trust him.

Alaric shared a meaningful look with his sentries, all three of them stone faced, eyes blazing, "We won't let that happen."

I let go of Alaric's hand, allowing the anger to seep back in, "Find Edris. Bring him to me."

I sat in the parlor, awaiting Edris' arrival. Alaric stood at my side, and Thana lounged in an armchair. Kade left to continue following Selbi, and Finn returned to the library.

My mood had brightened tenfold since leaving my bedchamber. Darius had been hard at work while I slept. The room looked nothing like it had before. Thick, luscious curtains in shades of blue, purple, and silver draped every window. Dark plush carpets covered the floor, and every piece of furniture was reupholstered to match the tasteful summers-night décor.

I couldn't wait to see him, so I could thank him. He would return soon with the decorator to complete the task since no one would allow him entry into my bedchamber.

Not moments after I sat down, still weakened from the cere-mony, Edris arrived, following a servant into the room. He seemed rattled by the change in décor, and I wondered if the ghastly white was his idea, or if the King Consort even spent much time in the royal chambers.

He came back to himself, regarding me with a delicate stare, "Liana," he breathed, as if he'd only just noticed my presence, "Are you alright? I—we've been worried about you."

"Have you?" I challenged, reigning in the urge to lash out at him like a petulant child.

Edris had the decency to be taken aback at my question, his thick brows dipping low over his eyes. "Of course, I have," he countered, taking a few more steps forward. "It wasn't me who instigated the petition to be put into power, if that's what this is about. I wouldn't attempt to dethrone my own daughter."

"Oh, but you would send me away to live on that godsfor-saken island for twenty-three years. And you would have left me there longer, hundreds of years maybe, if Enya hadn't fallen." I couldn't help it, I was *fuming*.

His hands balled into fists at his sides, "That was for your protection. There have already been two attempts on your life since your return. Do you not think it was wise of us to send you away—to—to send you somewhere *safe?*"

"One," Alaric said, and it took me a moment to understand what he meant, "There was only one attempt on Liana's life, and the wraith's can't get to her on dry land... unless there's another incident you know of?"

No one outside of my captain and sentries knew someone tried to poison me. Well, only them and Rin, who was guarded at all times. *And the person responsible,* I thought, and watched as Edris' face registered shock before it reverted to confusion. "One, yes, that's what I said."

He was lying. And I was either about to do something incredibly stupid, or incredibly smart.

"You were right the first time. There *were* two attempts on my life. It's a good thing Alaric detected the scent of verbane in my wine or I'd be dead."

Thana gasped, "And you didn't tell me of this?"

"No, you only would have worried."

"You should have told me," she fussed, leaving the parlor to get some air on the balcony.

Thana was there when I nearly died as a child from eating the poisonous berries, but not she, nor any of the sisters knew I continued to eat them well into adolescence, and often snacked on them during my walks about the isle.

Edris produced an air of concern, his lips turning downward into a frown. "Have you caught the person responsible?" he asked.

"No. And my taster is very thorough, I can't imagine how she missed it. Though I trust her not to make the same mistake twice."

Alaric cleared his throat, a habit I now knew was born of nerves, but he said nothing.

"Is there anything I can do to help?" Edris offered, his steady gaze betraying nothing. He was good. *Too good.* I wondered how old he was, and how long he'd had to become adapted to the trickery and scheming that was life at the palace.

I stood, the crown weighing me like a boulder atop my head, "You can keep this knowledge to yourself. No one outside of this room should know. And if you meant what you said, I trust you to see to it that this *petition* to place you in power is overthrown."

I watched his adams apple bob when he swallowed and painted on a mask of determination. "I will, Liana."

"And Edris," I called after him before he could depart, "You may address me from now on with my proper title."

Alaric waited for the sound of the main door closing behind Edris before he spoke, his tone laced with fury, "Explain yourself."

CHAPTER TWELVE

*A*fter rushing Thana from the room, I explained to Alaric what I had done. He didn't agree with me at first, but eventually relented. It was done. There was no taking it back. Though Alaric made it clear he would behead Edris himself and be done with it.

He was convinced Edris was behind the attempts on my life, and though I wasn't yet certain, I was leaning toward agreeing with him.

But the Night Court adored the King Consort. We couldn't eliminate him without causing uproar. At least, not until we could provide proof...

If Edris was behind the assassination attempts and thought we suspected him, he would sever all ties to his accomplices and find other means to get rid of me. But if he thought I trusted him with information—and if he thought I trusted my taster, and that I was susceptible to verbane, he may try the same tactic again. And we would be ready when he did.

"You're reckless," Alaric murmured once I had finished, "*Too* reckless. Please include me in your decision making from here on, at least as it pertains to your safety."

I would make no promises, but I nodded.

"You should rest," he said, rising from the settee with a stretch and a yawn. "I'll tell the council you are well and will address the court tomorrow."

I stood, shaking my head, "You're the one who needs to rest. Am I wrong to assume you haven't slept since the ceremony?"

He didn't answer.

"I'm going to the library to help Finn, and I'll be there for as long as it takes to figure *this* out," I said, drawing air circles around my eyes. "And while I'm doing that, I'd like it if you rested."

Alaric pressed his lips together in a slight frown, bowing low, a mocking tone to his voice when he said, "Yes, Your *Majesty*. If that will please you."

I shoved his chest when he rose, catching him off guard. He stumbled backward a step before regaining his balance and clearing his throat. "Don't *Your Majesty* me. Have you seen your reflection? You look terrible. I'm doing you a favor," I joked, tearing the crown from my head and tossing it onto a cushioned ottoman. "Now, shall we?"

We weren't in the corridor for more than a few moments when Selbi came into view, walking toward the royal quarters. Kade was no where to be seen, but that didn't mean he wasn't following somewhere out of sight.

"Oh, Your Majesty," she said, speaking in my presence for what I thought was the first time, "I was so glad to hear you'd recovered. The kitchens were just preparing your evening meal, and I thought I would taste—"

"Very good." I cut her off mid-ramble, and noted how her cheeks inflamed before she could bow her head, "I'll not be returning to my quarters for a while, but please, go ahead without me. I'll dine when I return."

"Yes, majesty," she squeaked out, taking off at a near run down the corridor.

Before she was out of sight, Kade appeared before us.

"Watch the taster closely," Alaric barked at Kade before he could open his mouth to greet us. "Liana took it upon herself to stir the pot. Make note of everything she does, and everywhere she goes. I'll explain later."

Kade winked at me before he combusted into a cloud of smoke and disappeared. "Did he just…" *Did he just disappear?*

Alaric clucked his tongue, "Such a showman," he teased, "Useful trick, though."

"You think?"

What I wouldn't give to be invisible too.

ALARIC LEFT me at the entrance to the library, having seen the back of Finn, hunched over a heaping pile of texts from across the room. He muttered something about needing to keep tabs on Edris even though I specifically said I wanted him to rest. He left before I could argue, squeezing my hand before dropping it quickly—but not quickly enough. Desire and apprehension crashed over me like a rogue wave into a tidal pool. I didn't have time to wonder if he'd done it on purpose, or if he ever accidentally pushed his own emotions through to others with his Grace.

Finn spun in his chair as though he could sense me standing there even though I hadn't made a sound.

"Your Majesty," he said by way of greeting, "Where's Alaric?"

"Resting, I hope." I pulled out the chair across from him at the long table, overwhelmed at the amount of parchment before me. "Have you found anything?"

He ran a hand over the scruff on his jawline, "No. Nothing really. There was this one scroll though," he lamented, digging through a pile of parchment on the right of the table, "Ah, here."

I took it from his outstretched hand. It was ancient—written in the language of old, marking it as being aged around five hundred years.

"I can only read bits and pieces. I've been teaching myself Melîn, but I haven't mastered it yet."

Lucky for him, I *could* read it. Thana thought it would be a useful language to know, since there were still some Fae—who lived in the villages far to the north, who still spoke it. I studied the scroll, squinting at the faded looping script. It was written by a scribe and documented the Blessing Ceremony of Morgana. It was a copy, then. Every few centuries the scribes who worked in the archives copied the older scrolls before they could become tattered and illegible.

This was from before Morgana was crowned, and that was likely why it wasn't in the royal archives—even though at the time, Morgana was still the daughter of the King.

Though, if Thana was right, they *changed* with each copy. Like the whisper game I loved to play as a child where the seven sisters and I would sit in a circle. I would whisper something to the sister next to me, and she would repeat it to the next and so on. By the time it reached the seventh, and they spoke it out loud, it would be something entirely different—and usually funny.

"It documents Morgana's Blessing Ceremony," I told Finn.

"That much I gathered. But it was this part here that caught my eye." Finn came around the table and leaned in over my shoulder to point out a section of text about halfway down the page.

I read it aloud, translating as I went, "The results of Morgana's Ceremony were indeterminable." I narrowed my eyes at the scroll, "But Morgana was Graced with fire, wasn't she?" I asked Finn.

"Keep reading."

"The ground shook not a moment after she drank of the

Sidhe. She feinted and was carried from the Great Hall by His Royal Majesty, King Ricon II." *The Mad King.*

I set the scroll back down on the table, "Do you think my Grace is fire then? Like hers?"

"That was not her only Grace," a scribe who was putting tomes and scrolls back to their places on the many shelves said, turning to address us. "Your Majesty," he said bowing. The male was thick around the middle, and *old*. It was strange to see someone who looked beyond the mortal age of thirty, with wrinkles and silver in their hair. Very rare, but it had been known to happen—where a Fae didn't complete their transformation until later in life.

"There was a scroll once, many years ago that described Morgana on the front-lines of battle at Mount Noctis. The scribe detailed her charge into battle and wrote how he witnessed the queen-to-be use the Graces of air, strength, and earth as well as her documented Grace of fire."

I had never heard that story before and was sure it was one Thana would have told me. She always told me tales of Morgana to soothe me to sleep. "And where is this scroll? In the royal archives?"

The old scribe huffed, "You won't find it now, majesty. It was lost long ago."

Well that's helpful.

"Though," he said, "I suspect you may find what you're looking for in the royal chambers. It was Morgana who had those chambers built, surely there are answers to be found within."

Finn and I shared a look. "What do you—" I started, but the scribe was gone. Vanished.

Finn shrugged his shoulders, "What do you suppose he meant?"

"I have no idea."

After coming up empty handed, Finn escorted me back to my chambers. "There must be something," he said, exasperated. "Perhaps, if you would give permission, I could look through the royal archives?"

"Of course."

His lips twitched up into a bashful half smile, and he looked at me as though he was only now seeing me for the first time. "Maj—"

"Liana," I corrected, and his smile grew.

Where his brother was all cheeky grins, and sly stares, Finn was intense. He held me captive in his pensive gaze and didn't seem to speak unless it was to say something intelligent. A philosopher trapped in the toned and deadly body of a Horde warrior.

A beautiful combination of strength and wit.

I don't know why I hadn't noticed before.

"Liana," he intoned, as if tasting my name on his tongue, and enjoying the flavor, "I wanted to apologize."

"For what?"

He looked to the floor, and I noticed frost form along the ridges of his knuckles. *Ice.* One brother of flame and the other of frost. How fitting. "For not being around as much as my brother, or Alaric. I—well I requested duties that would keep me away. You see, I'm not used to being around—"

"Royalty?" I offered.

"Females."

"Oh."

I didn't even realize I'd stopped walking until Finn was a few steps ahead of me and I jogged to catch up. "I didn't realize," I started. It was hard to picture that either of the twins wouldn't be accustomed to being around females. I knew of the brothels in around the Horde camp, and there was no way the two of them wouldn't be well-attended there. As if their looks weren't enough, they were Draconian.

I knew, at least for me, that would make them even more appealing. They were rare. *Exotic.*

"Consider it forgiven," I told him, waiting for him to lift his head before I finished, "And in case you didn't know, it was only a week ago that I first *saw* a male, let alone spoke to one, or had one guarding me as I slept."

"Oh."

We cleared the rest of the corridor, my arm looped through his, and rounded the bend to my royal chambers, "Don't worry, Finn. We'll both figure it out, eventually."

He laughed, and the sound was one which started deep in his belly and made me want to laugh too.

It was nice to know I wasn't the only one getting used to new things.

CHAPTER THIRTEEN

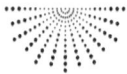

"*A*laric?" I exclaimed, walking into my chamber, Finn and I subduing our outburst of laughter.

Alaric raised his eyebrows at us, and I thought I saw his jaw tighten, "I rested, as requested. I've come to relieve Finn," he said, sharing a tense look with his sentry.

"I can stay—" Finn started.

Alaric shook his head, "That's alright. I need you to shadow Edris. We think he might be—"

"I'm just going to wash up," I interrupted, before Alaric could tell Finn what I had done earlier that day. *Would he agree with me, I wondered? Or like Alaric, would he think it unwise?* I didn't care to know.

I left the pair in the entryway, eager to feel clean after days spent in bed and hours spent pouring over dusty tomes in the library.

The water was luxurious, heated to perfection and infused with lavender and jasmine brought to the palace from southern traders. The oils made my skin feel like silk, and the warmth soothed my body, but did little to temper my thoughts.

I knew it would take time for my Grace to develop, and even

more time still for me to learn how to use it. But every Graced Fae got a small taste of their new power during the Ceremony. They knew what to look for—what to expect. I didn't.

I wasn't even certain I was Graced at all... unless my Grace was having eyes able to change color. I hadn't looked in the mirror since I awoke, but Finn told me they seemed to have settled between only changing from blue to violet and back again. *Whatever* that *means.*

"Are you alright?" Alaric's strained voice came through the wooden door.

"Fine!" I called back, sighing, "I'll be out in a moment."

It was maddening having to be guarded at all times. The hour I had spent in the bathing room was no where near enough. I had spent hours each day alone with my own thoughts, free to roam the isle as I pleased. I'd traded one cage for another, and I still wasn't convinced it was an improvement.

Don't do this, Liana. Don't do that, Liana. That's improper, Liana. Act like a queen, Liana.

Maddening.

With the plush robe staving off the chill wafting in from the tall window, I strode from the bathing room—and ran straight into Alaric's chest.

He caught me, "Whoa, there, what's the rush?"

I didn't step away, instead twisting in his arms to see his face. His breath caught, and his jaw clenched. I was still dripping wet, covered in nothing but the soft robe. Everywhere his hands touched me tingled.

I tilted my face up and his body tensed around me.

His grey eyes locked onto mine, and I noticed a ring of dark blue around his iris', and streaks of near-white and specks of black. His dark hair fell forward as he leaned in, chest rising to meet mine as he took a deep, steadying breath.

"Liana, I—," he started, trying to detangle himself from me, but I clutched him tighter, trying not to think about the consequences of what I was about to do.

"Stop thinking," I told him, watching as a war raged beneath the surface of his skin. I placed a hand on his bare shoulder, "Feel. Don't think."

He shuddered at my touch and a flash of carnal desire raced through me. I moaned, eyes closing and body melting at the feel of the raw emotion. My heart was a riot of thunder in my chest —a tempest that wouldn't calm.

A ferocious growl tore from his chest, and my eyes flew open. His warm hand wrapped around the soft flesh at the nape of my neck, tangling in my still-damp hair. He pulled gently, and it was enough to make my legs buckle.

His lips collided with mine as though there wasn't a second to waste. His kiss deepened, and he pressed his body against mine. I moaned again at the feel of his bulge pressing against me. The heat spread between us, enveloping me, expanding, contracting—settling into a blaze deep at my core. His tongue flicked against mine and a tremor scrambled down my spine.

"I knew it!" A shrill voice broke me out of the trance, and Alaric spun on his heel, hand on the hilt of his sword.

Thana stood across the room, seeming to have let herself in without the courtesy of knocking. Her hands gripped her hips, and the look she gave me could burn a hundred forests to the ground. "Thana!" I shouted, "What are you doing in here?"

She rolled her eyes, and instead of answering, she extended a hand, her fingers pulling at the air in the room.

"Thana don't—"

But it was too late, my air Graced handmaiden had already blown Alaric from the room. I watched him crash to the ground on the other side of the door before she used her Grace to slam that on his groaning form.

"What did you do that for?" I demanded.

"For your own good!"

Alaric came through the door, glaring at Thana, his eyes filling with malice.

"And *you*," she chastised, pointing a long finger at him, "You should know better."

I shook my head, falling into the chair beside my dressing table. "Thana calm down," I said.

Thana came to stand at my side, and I had to resist the urge to strangle her, "You may go. I will stay with the queen tonight."

He stiffened, clearing his throat, "It isn't safe. I'll stay."

Alaric searched my face, looking for something there, but I wasn't sure what. "It's alright Alaric," I told him, turning to face the mirror, "I'll be fine with Thana until morning."

Turning on his heel, he stormed from my bedchamber. I flinched when I heard the main door slam behind him.

CHAPTER FOURTEEN

*T*hat night, I was restless—falling asleep only to awaken again and again. I stepped from the comfort of my bed, cringing when my bare feet met the night-chilled tile. Thana was asleep in the armchair at the corner of the room. *Some bodyguard.*

I had planned to get a glass of water but found myself at the main door instead. I opened it in infinitesimal increments, afraid to wake Thana. She slept like the dead most times, but on edge as she was, I wouldn't risk it.

The palace was silent, not even the mice had come out of their holes in the walls. I crept on light feet through the corridors and down the spiral staircase into the ballroom. My heart thudded behind my breast and a cool sweat broke out along my collarbone.

Where was I going?

A pull at the core of my being drew me to the right, toward the Great Hall. I swallowed, eager to return to my chambers, but I was almost there. And there was *something* I had to see there... or something I had to do. I wasn't sure. In a trancelike state I padded to the entryway of the hall.

The cauldron perched atop its pedestal on the dais, beckoning. The bluish fog always rising from the surface of the water seemed to glow—almost to shimmer, small shining flecks catching the moonlight from where it streamed in from the windows on either side of the space.

Liana... a strange voice whispered, and I whirled around, searching for the owner of the voice. There was no one.

My lips parted, and I stood perfectly still, waiting for whoever it was to come out. Did someone lure me there? Was this all some form of trickery to get me out into the open? Alone. Did I fall for it?

I crept forward, keeping my eyes and ears open in case of an attack, cursing myself for not bringing a weapon with me—for leaving my chambers at all.

As I neared, it was clear the buckling of the earth I felt beneath me during my Ceremony was no hallucination. There was a jagged, crater-like dent in the marble where I had stood, and a fissure sliced through the stairs and spider-webbed out through the Great Hall.

Liana, the phantom voice whispered again, the sound seemed to come from everywhere and no where at the same time. I ground my teeth, wrapping my hands into the fabric of my night clothes.

I had to go back. I shouldn't have ventured so far from the safety of my chambers alone. But I was almost there—almost standing over the cauldron of water that almost destroyed me.

The fog thickened and pulsed as if it were a living thing. The air cooled to the point of freezing until plumes of steam accentuated my rapid breathing.

Be warned... the voice said, echoing inside my skull. *Not everything is as it seems...*

I wrapped my arms around myself to stave off the chill, speaking through chattering teeth, "Wha—what do you mean? Who are you?"

Liana...

"What do you want?"

A crash outside the Great Hall had me snapping my attention to the entrance, my heart galloping in my chest.

Run, the voice commanded, and a section of the wall opened behind the cauldron, warm air pouring from the darkness within. The sound of thudding footfalls heading straight for the Great Hall thundered from across the room. Without time to think, I flung myself into the hidden passageway and the stone door shut behind me.

The darkness was all-consuming. It was as though someone had thrown me into a vat of ink. The air was musty and warm and the floor slick with condensation. I shuddered, stabilizing myself with a hand on the rough stone wall as I stood. I listened for a sound, for anything, but was met with complete and utter silence.

If there was a way in, there must be a way out, I told myself, cursing my rash decision to jump inside. I pressed lightly against the wall where the hidden doorway had been, but somehow, I knew, I just *knew* it wasn't safe on the other side any longer. Whoever had been about to enter the Great Hall wished me harm. And that voice, whatever—or whoever it was—was trying to protect me.

Swallowing my panic, I searched for another means of escape, using the walls of tunnel-like corridor to find my way.

WHAT FELT like hours could've only been minutes as I followed the path around a sharp corner and saw a faint fissure of light up ahead. *A way out!* I raced to it, using my nails to pry open the section of wall. In my haste to break free of the blackness, I tripped, falling to my knees on the other side. The entrance sealed itself back into place behind me.

if the scent of lilac and rosebud was any indication, I was

near the gardens. The passageway I'd just come out of had vanished. Only if I looked closely, could I see the near imperceptible line in the otherwise smooth stone wall.

I flew from the alcove, ready to run straight back to my bed, when a shadowy figure emerged from the gardens.

"Who's there?" he shouted.

And I ran. I ran as fast as I could but didn't get more than a few paces when I was tackled to the ground. He knocked the air from my lungs, and I struggled to breath. The male had me pinned to the ground, his hands like manacles around my wrists, his body weight pressing into my hips.

I thrashed and struggled, vaguely aware of the strangled sounds escaping my lips. The male was off me within an instant, staggering backwards.

"Queen Liana?" he asked, though it was more of a statement. He fell to one knee, bowing his head, his honey blonde hair looking more like muted beige in the bright moonlight. "Please forgive me."

"Tiernan?"

What is he doing out here all alone in the middle of the night? And without a guard.

He looked up, and I saw the strain in his sharp features, "Please," he repeated, "I didn't know it was you."

I stood, brushing the dust from nightclothes. "Why are you out here? Why are you even still here at all?"

He arose, flipping his hair back away from his face, "It calms me," he said, "When I can't sleep, it's soothing to be outdoors."

I hurried to cover the exposed flesh of my breasts, tying the lace at my collar tighter with shaking fingers.

Tiernan only then seemed to notice my lack of attire, and averted his gaze, "Are you alright, majesty?"

I rolled my eyes at him. *Does it* look *like I'm alright? No. I couldn't sleep and was propelled into the Great Hall where I hallucinated hearing voices and was nearly attacked only to be locked in a*

dark passageway and finally find my out only to be assaulted by you!
"I'm fine."

"You're bleeding," he said, coming near.

I took a step back in response.

"I won't hurt you," he said, his voice gentle, as though speaking to a cornered mutt. He pulled a length of cloth from the pocket of his trousers, "Let me wrap it for you. And then we'll get you back to your chambers."

Now that he'd drawn attention to it, I could feel the sting on my right knee, throbbing with each rapid beat of my heart. It would heal fast, as wounds did once the transformation from mortal to immortal was complete.

"Why are you helping me?"

"Why not? We're alone out here, who else is there to help you? Or would you not do the same for someone you saw in distress?"

I couldn't help it, I blurted, "Don't you despise the Night Court? Isn't that—I don't know, like bred into you?"

He chuckled, and the sound pulled at something inside my chest. When he came forward again, I didn't move away. He knelt in front of me, tearing the cloth into two pieces to wrap around my wound. "There's been tension between our two courts for centuries—millennia actually, since the Mad King divided the land, but no, it isn't *bred* into us. Though the older of the Fae in my court uphold that you lot are all a scheming, selfish sort of folk and are not to be trusted."

"And you?" I asked, wincing as he secured the makeshift bandage into place with a tight knot.

He rose to my eye level, and I averted my gaze, so the darkness could hide the roiling colors of my iris'. "I think there is good and bad in everyone—and we should not uphold the prejudices of our ancestors."

"Thank you," I said, gesturing to my now bandaged knee.

He bowed, "You're welcome."

He cocked his head, and I realized he was staring into my eyes, "Your eyes, they're different."

I turned away, and he took my arm, spinning me back around to face him. I parted my lips to shout at him and found his bright green ones not more than an inch from my own. "They're beautiful. They seem brighter in the moonlight."

My heart sped. There was wonder in his gaze, and I had to work to calm my erratic pulse.

How could something so beautiful be so dangerous?

I was about to tell him to let go of me, I *swear* I was, when a shadow fell upon us. The sound of beating wings was audible for a mere second before the Draconian barreled into Tiernan, sending him careening into the palace walls.

"Kade!" I shouted, thinking it to be him, but it was Finn who turned, eyes ringed with glowing yellow. "Stop!" I shouted at him before he could charge Tiernan again.

He came toward me, wings spread wide, his features softening and footfalls slowing when he beheld my ragged appearance. "Why are you alone? Did he hurt you?" Finn examined me for damage, a blush crawling up his neck.

I took his outstretched hand into my own, hoping to reassure him, "I'm alright. Tiernan found me, he—well he was helping me." I thought it wise to leave out the part where he tackled me first.

Finn turned to where Tiernan was lifting himself from the ground. The ease with which he stood made it appear as though the Draconian had merely shoved him. But the buckling stone behind him told the truth.

Finn retracted his wings, "I thought—"

Tiernan waved off his attempt at an apology, "No harm done. I would have thought the same."

Clasping Finn's hand, I led the warrior away, "Thank you," I called back to Tiernan. "And you can stay here at court as long as you like."

CHAPTER FIFTEEN

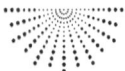

*a*laric was furious the next morning. Finn had stayed with me throughout the rest of the night after some harsh words exchanged with a very ashamed Thana.

"I knew I shouldn't have left!" he exclaimed, running a fisted hand through his still-tousled hair. "And what were you doing out alone in the middle of the night, anyway? With everything that's happened, Liana..." he groaned, "It isn't safe."

I was glad I had time to remove the bandage from my knee, clean the blood from the skin and change into a clean gown before he arrived, or he would have been even more in distress at my appearance.

"And invited the emissary to *stay*? Why would you do that?"

I was seething, but I knew he had good intentions, and only wanted my safety. "I'm sorry. I just—I had to see it—the Great Hall, and the cauldron. It was like it was calling me," I said, reigning in the urge to lash out.

He looked at me with patronizing eyes, making me want to cry out with frustration, "Calling to you?" he asked, as though I'd said the most ridiculous thing in the world.

And maybe I had. Maybe it was all a strange dream my

stress-addled mind created to play tricks on me. But that couldn't be true. I *had* gone there, and I *had* heard a voice—a voice that warned me and told me to run and had kept me safe from whoever had been coming to harm me. It didn't matter if Alaric didn't believe me.

"I'm sorry," he said, calmer, coming to rub warmth into my shoulders, "What's important is you're alright."

I nodded.

He sighed, and I relaxed into his embrace, "I'm sorry I frightened you."

"I'm sorry I shouted."

Kade came in then, raising his eyebrows at the sight of Alaric and me, still locked together.

"Captain," he said, jaw tensing, "Silas has requested to meet with you."

The Captain of the Horde armies? I wondered what for.

"Right," Alaric digressed, releasing me from his embrace, and taking his time about it too. "I'll be back soon. Stay with Kade."

Once he was out of sight, Kade rushed me, lifting me in a tight hug so my feet dangled a foot from the ground. I gasped. "It's only fair." He winked. *Cocky bastard.* "The three of us share everything. The fearsome threesome—that's what they called us back at camp."

"Surely you didn't share *everything*," I mused, disentangling my limbs from his.

He tilted his head to one side, pursed his lips, nodded, "Most things, yes."

I dropped back to the floor and steadied myself with a hand on his bicep, "Females?"

Waggling his eyebrows at me he said with a wolfish grin, "Sometimes."

"So, none of you are bonded, then?"

Kade made a dismissive sound at the thought, "No," he said, sounding as though he was stating the obvious, "But...

we are all bound to you. Not by magic, but by honor and duty."

That beautiful, warm ache spread through me again. I bit my lower lip to keep it from trembling at the thought of the three males. All bound to me. *Mine.* Kade followed the motion with hungry eyes, "Why are you looking at me like that?"

His wings whipped out from his back and his eyes darkened, filling with lust. The room heated, and I knew if I touched him, it would burn—but I wouldn't care. "Don't ask me questions you already know the answers to."

THE SPARRING COURTYARD was twice the size of the ballroom, closed in on all sides by thick stone walls, the ground made up of soft, dark sand. It took several splashes of cool water before I was ready to leave my chambers with Kade. It was my sugges-tion, if only to clear my head and get out of the privacy of my chambers. I wasn't sure if I could restrain myself.

I wanted him. And I wanted Alaric. Finn was just as beau-tiful as his brother, but with a quiet grace I desired too. They were mine. But was I ready to make myself theirs? The nobles would consider it *improper* to take more than one lover. They couldn't *all* be King Consort after all. But why should I have to choose?

Della, one of the seven sisters on the isle was skilled in the art of combat and gave me a little training. Not enough to stand up against Kade, but that wasn't why we were here. Spread evenly throughout the sandy circle were three short pedestals. Atop one sat a stone bowl, a fire burning inside. The second was filled with water. And the third held a bounty of blossoming flower buds. Hay-filled sacks in the vague shape of bodies stood in a line around the room.

This courtyard, though also used for traditional combat sparring, was made for newly Graced Fae to develop their abilities. Since I didn't yet know what my Grace was, it seemed the logical place to start.

"Finn said it could be fire," mused Kade, "Like me."

"It could be. Can you show me how it works?"

Kade opened his hands, raising them from his sides so I could see, "Your Grace comes from inside you. It's a part of you. When I first trained, only certain things would trigger it. Like if I was angry," he said, and a ball of flame appeared in his hand, hovering just above his flesh, "Or if I was turned on," he continued, tipping his head toward me, his other hand igniting with flame, "Now, it's as easy as breathing, I call for it, and it comes."

I tried to imagine a force inside me like Kade described, and tried to draw it out, but nothing happened.

"You aren't trying hard enough," he told me, the flames in his palms evaporating into small clouds of smoke. "Use your emotions. Think of something that makes you angry."

Sighing, I did as instructed and thought of Edris, and of my mother, and about the Blessing Ceremony. I thought I felt something stir within me, but then I thought about the assembly I'd have to address later that afternoon, and worry won out over rage.

"Hmmm," Kade stroked his jaw, "Maybe..." he trailed off, and then swung his arms in a wide arc around me, setting the sand at my feet ablaze. I jumped back, but tripped, my hand falling into the fire. I yelped, and then as quickly as the flames appeared, they disappeared in a cloud of smoke.

Kade rushed over, cursing, and grabbed my hand to inspect my fingers. "You weren't supposed to fall!"

The skin on my first three fingers was red, but otherwise unharmed. Kade dropped it back to my side, scrunching his face.

"What?" I asked.

He reached up and placed a hand on my neck, sending my thoughts elsewhere, "Tell me if this hurts," he said, and I felt his hand warm on my neck, then grow hot. After a moment more it was near burning and I yanked it off.

"That's odd," he said while probing my neck with his now cool fingers, "If your Grace was fire, it shouldn't have hurt you at all. *But*, that was enough heat to melt metal, and it only reddened your skin."

"That's good, right? My Grace could just be developing and that's why it hurt."

Fire! I was Graced with Fire. It was an honorable Grace and one the denizens of my court would approve of.

"Maybe," Kade relented, "But maybe not. I could try something else to see if your Grace reacts..."

"Alright."

Kade's fingers ceased probing my already healing wound and wound themselves around my neck. He jerked me forward, crushing his mouth against mine. His other hand grasped my waist and hoisted me onto him.

I yelped in surprise before letting the sensation take over. A fire ignited up my spine, and I kissed him back greedily, the *need* outweighing any sane thought in my mind. He caught my lower lip between his teeth and I whimpered, my hips moving against him of their own accord. He growled in response, tensed—and then dropped me.

I was dizzy on my feet, lightheaded and trying to regain control of my body. The burning between my legs subsided with each short breath.

"Well," he said between pants, smirking, his eyes glazed with a sheen of carnal desire, glowing around the edges. "That didn't work."

CHAPTER SIXTEEN

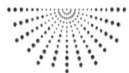

*T*he assembly was mostly made up of nobles, courtesans and council members, but I found the faces of a few townsfolk among them. In the front stood Edris, looking regal in white trousers, with a deep purple tunic embroidered in gold. Near him stood Ronan, his jaw set in a grimace, and Silas, the Captain of the Horde armies.

My skin bristled at so many eyes staring up at me. Alaric was at my side on the dais in the Great Hall, hands clasped behind his back. And when I turned to look at him, he gave me an encouraging nod. I kept my eyes downcast as instructed, even though Thana styled my hair to swoop low over my forehead, concealing the ever-changing colors in shadow.

Until we knew what it meant, we had all agreed it was best to keep it hidden.

"I apologize for being absent these past days," I began, not remembering what to say, even though Thana had drilled the words into me over and over when Kade and I returned from the sparring courtyard. "I was taking rest in my chambers but can assure all of you I am well."

Tiernan caught my eye, standing alone in the corner of the

hall, close to the dais. His gaze travelled the length of me, making my stomach tighten. Darius had designed me another gown, this one silver, fitted, with a deep 'V' shape cut into the front. It was beautiful, and comfortable, but also the most revealing thing I'd ever worn. *Keep their attention here,* he had said with a wink before I left to address the assembly, *and they'll forget why they're even there.*

It seemed, in Tiernan's case at least, Darius' trick had worked.

"Were you Graced?" one of the nobles near the front of the room asked outright, a few others around him whispering and nodding.

I was prepared for that question, Thana had given me the perfect response, something that would neither confirm, nor deny anything—but the words eluded me, and I froze.

"Why did the water cause you pain?" another noble shouted from somewhere else.

And yet another shouted, "Why is the emissary still among us? Send him away!"

I clenched my jaw, wanting desperately to hold on to something sturdy. "I—well, I—"

I realized then how neither of the questioners addressed me with the proper title. I bit the inside of my cheek to regain control. And I was about to command silence from the crowd when Edris stepped forward and the people hushed.

"The *queen* was only Graced just days ago. Surely you all remember how long it took to control your Grace?"

"If she has one," I heard someone say, but couldn't decipher who'd said it.

Edris stood tall, his jaw set, "Rest assured, she was Graced. Our queen simply needs time."

Time, yes, I need time. But for now, the people had to know *I* was in control. That *I* would not go quietly. And I didn't need to be pitied or protected by someone who would rather have the crown for himself.

"Enough," I seethed, hands turning to claws at my sides.

Edris spun to find me glaring at him from the dais. His mouth clamped shut.

Liana...

The phantom voice sent a shiver up my spine, and I turned to see fog spill over the cauldron. Alaric stood still, cocking his head at me. I shook off the tremors. "This absurd questioning is over," I told them all, turning back and attempting to make eye contact with each of the Fae in attendance.

Liana... it whispered again, *run my child, you are not safe within these walls.*

Alaric still showed no sign he'd heard anything.

Stop it, I directed the thought at the cauldron, *leave me alone.*

"You heard the queen. This assembly is over," Alaric echoed from my side, showing force with a hand curled around the hilt of his sword.

CHAPTER SEVENTEEN

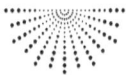

"$\mathcal{W}$hat do we do?" I whined, falling backward into my bed, my hands covering my eyes, "If I can't prove I'm Graced soon, they'll—"

Alaric sat next to me, "You *will* prove it. And in the meantime, we'll keep you safe—whatever it takes."

The truth was, if it was only a matter of passing the crown on to someone else, I would consider it... but it was my duty to ensure the safety of my court, and to make sure the person ruling it was worthy. And once the crown was out of my hands, the nobles would want my head too. They would want to put an end to my bloodline. An ungraced queen would be too likely to produce an ungraced heir someday.

"I have another bit of bad news."

I groaned, "What now?"

Alaric pressed a small rolled scroll into the palm of my hand, "We caught the emissary trying to send this scroll by falcon. It holds the royal seal of the Day Court."

Shooting up, I beheld the scroll. The wax seal was green, and showed a tree, its roots long and interwoven, but instead of leaves and branches, this tree held the sun atop its trunk. A

letter meant for the queen. The seal hadn't yet been broken—
and couldn't be. Neither Tiernan, nor the Queen of the Day
Court would take to kindly to knowing their private correspon-
dence was tampered with.

"What do you suppose it says?"

Alaric threw his hands up, "Your guess is as good as mine.
But it can't be good. Either it's an account of what happened at
your Blessing Ceremony, or it's an account of the dissent among
your people. Those are the types of things he would report on."

"Or it's both." I mused, wanting to toss the scroll into the
fireplace across the room. "Suriel cannot know my court is in
turmoil. We still can't be certain they're to blame for the assassination of Enya—or the attempt on my life, but if they are..." I
trailed off.

"Then now would be the perfect time to strike," Alaric
finished for me.

He stood, pacing the room, "I'll need more sentries," he said,
head bent in concentration. "The three of us—it isn't enough to
protect you. And Silas is growing impatient, with three more
nobles gone missing, he wonders why I haven't brought the
councils selected sentries for your approval."

"And why haven't you?"

"Because I don't trust the council."

"Nor do I," I exhaled, dragging myself back into a seated
position, "Turn them down," I told him, "It will take time for
them to select new candidates, and while they're busy doing
that, hire sentries of your own, ones you can trust. We can call
them... temporary fill-ins—to placate the council for now."

Alaric nodded, "Alright."

"And select someone to guard Tiernan as well."

"Tiernan?" he asked, brow furrowed.

I swallowed, "Yes, Tiernan. The Day Court emissary."

Until he leaves, he isn't safe here either.

Alaric stopped pacing, glaring down at me, "I suppose he

can't leave—knowing all he does. We can't allow him to share that information with Suriel."

That was not the reason I thought to keep him guarded, more so worried about his safety. There was something about him I couldn't put my finger on. A likeness, perhaps? He seemed to understand me—my motives in inviting him. And to share my feelings about the tension between our two courts, and how unfounded it was. I wanted him safe, nothing more. And I wouldn't hold him back if he requested to leave. But Alaric didn't need to know that.

Wait, what was that he'd said? About more missing nobles. "Wait, did you say more nobles have disappeared?"

He nodded, running a fisted hand through his dark hair, "It seems so. Three more that we know of, including Silas' own sister."

"Any idea where they could have gone?"

"Not yet, but Silas has sent scouts to search for them as far north as the edge of the Wastes. I'm sure they'll find them." But he didn't look so certain—he appeared worried and avoided looking me in the eyes.

"Now, about that letter..." he said, sitting back down next to me, his leg brushing against mine, sending a delicious shiver down my spine. "What would you like me to do?"

"Nothing. I'll keep it—for now."

And I would keep it... until I could speak to Tiernan myself and decipher its contents.

I knew Alaric would never allow such a thing, but Kade, my devious and daring Kade, just might help me.

WITH ALARIC EAGER TO find trustworthy sentries to add to the Royal Guard, I didn't have to wait long for Kade to relieve him. The Draconian warrior looked opposing in the otherwise delicately decorated parlour. He was a mass of muscle covered in black leathers, his wings tucked tightly into his back.

"Spit it out," he said, moving one of this game pieces into a slot on the board that would only lead to his downfall. "I know you want to ask me something, you've been biting your lips for the past hour."

I set my game piece into position to destroy the one he moved a moment ago, eliciting a groan from his lips, "I need you to do something for me."

"And what's that?"

"I need you to take me to see Tiernan."

He lost his focus on the game, raising a quizzical gaze to meet mine, "What for?"

I pressed my lips shut.

Kade made a noncommittal sound and leaned back onto the settee, "If you won't tell me, that means Alaric won't like it. And if Alaric doesn't like it, then I'll be on the hook for it when whatever *it* is blows up in your face."

"It's important," I told him, and waited for him to reconsider, his lips pursed and muscles flexing.

Finally, he cocked his head to the side, regarding me with eyes aglow, "What do I get out of it?"

I opened my hands, "Whatever you want."

Kade growled, "I'd be careful what you offer me, Liana," he said, eyeing my curves, making my skin tingle and prickle with heat. "But I accept, and you can replay me *later*."

"You are wicked," I jested.

"The wickedest," he said, coy, "But you like it, don't you?"

CHAPTER EIGHTEEN

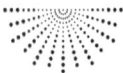

"Your Majesty," Tiernan exclaimed, opening the door to his chamber in nothing but a thin cotton undershirt and trousers unbuttoned at the top and hanging low, *very low.*

He pulled up his trousers and buttoned them, so they remained securely above his hips. "Hello," I said, "Sorry to intrude, I was hoping you had a moment to speak with me."

Tiernan brushed the blond hair from his face, looking so much less put together than I'd ever seen him. "Now?"

"Yes, now. May I come in?"

He straightened his cotton undershirt, blushing as he noticed it was all he was wearing. I could see each of the muscles of his abdomen through it, even in their latent forms. Tiernan waved an arm inside the room, "My chambers are you chambers, majesty."

Kade moved to follow me inside, but I stopped him with a look. "I'm in no danger here. You can wait outside." He muttered something about Alaric ripping him to pieces, but did as I asked, stationing himself outside the door as I closed it.

The emissary rushed to clear a chair of papers and remove a

half-empty crystal decanter from the table. He pulled the chair out for me, and I sat, folding my hands in front of me, the scroll clasped between my fingers.

Tiernan slumped into a chair opposite me, eyes fixed on the scroll, "I was wondering why he came back so quickly," he said gesturing to the falcon sitting on its perch by the window. It was a magnificent bird, with small black eyes and russet brown feathers. It watched me, tilting its head as though saying hello.

I twirled the school between my fingers, then tossed it into Tiernan's lap. He lifted it, bewildered to find the seal still intact.

"I didn't know my sentries had intercepted it," I told him, "And as you can see, I didn't read its contents."

"Why not?"

I shrugged, "I'd rather it if you told me what it says."

He raised an eyebrow at me, "And you would trust me to speak the truth?"

"Should I not?"

"No, you shouldn't," he told me, eyes darkening, "But not because it says what you think it does—but rather because you shouldn't trust anyone at court."

Without another word, he broke the seal, and rose to place the scroll into my hand, his fingers brushing the soft skin of my wrist. "Read it."

He wasn't lying, it didn't say what I thought it would. Written in a fine script was his account of my Ceremony—and it wasn't true.

It said I was Graced with fire, and the denizens of my court welcomed him and held their queen in high esteem. It also said he had been invited to stay and thought it would be a dishonor to refuse the offer.

"But this isn't true," I said, incredulous, "Why not tell her the truth? That my court is falling to ruin, and there has been no proof I was Graced at all? Is that not your duty?"

He considered my statement, taking the small piece of

parchment from my hands, "Perhaps. But it would do no good for her to know that—and I would like to see you keep your throne."

He poured himself a glass of wine from the decanter, looking at me in askance before he filled the second. I nodded. "But why? Why are you helping me?"

"The truth?"

"Yes, the truth."

He handed me the glass, and swirled the contents of his own, staring down into the rich crimson liquid as though it held all the answers, "Because I think you are a good person. And because I'd like to stay and learn more about your customs—I find the Night Court fascinating."

There was something else, but he hesitated before saying it, "And I'm curious," he said, casting a sly glance my way.

"Curious? About what?"

Tiernan took a long swallow of his wine, "About you. And about *that*," he told me, pointing at my face.

My eyes. I had forgotten to conceal them from him. *Stupid.*

Too late to deny it now.

"Do you know what it means?" I asked, thinking perhaps there was knowledge of the strange occurrence in the Day Court.

Solemnly, he shook his head, coming to kneel in front of me, "May I," he asked, but before I could answer he tucked a lock of hair behind my ear—away from my face, and tilted my chin down to look into his vivid sea-water eyes. "There is a story someone told me as a boy, that one day everything we knew would change. It would be the dawn of a new era... and there would be a queen, beautiful and fierce—the most powerful ever seen, who would rule us all."

My throat tightened at his words, and the way he beheld me, like a dragon guarding its horde. "It's a fable."

"Possibly," he acquiesced, "But there is truth to every tale,

Liana. And if there were to be only one queen who rose above the rest, I don't think it would be Suriel… it would be *you*."

"YOU DON'T BELIEVE HIM, do you?" Kade asked, his tone filled with skepticism.

I scowled at him, "Were you eavesdropping?"

"I was standing right outside the door," he said, and then, "Well, do you?"

"I'm not sure."

Kade grabbed my shoulder, spinning me to face him before we could enter my chambers, "It could be the Day Court that's responsible for the attempts on your life. You know that, right?"

I turned on him, yanking my shoulder from his grasp, "And you know he's only one person, and does not embody all the Day Court stands for, right? And you know he hadn't even arrived at court when my wine was poisoned. So, yes, I *do* believe him."

Alaric, having heard us in the corridor, flew from my chambers, the door clanging against the wall beside us. He didn't speak, but the fury in his eyes was enough to send me a few steps backward.

"Alaric—" Kade began, but Alaric silenced him with a well-aimed right hook, punching Kade in the jaw. He staggered backward, clutching his face, but made no move to retaliate. Alaric moved in to strike again, but I stood between the two, my chin raised to show I wouldn't be moving.

How Alaric found out where we were, I wasn't sure, but it was the only reason he could have to be so angry.

"Stop," I ordered. "It wasn't his fault. I made him do it."

Hurt darkened Alaric's features and dulled the normally bright silvery grey of his eyes. "You *asked* him to kiss you?"

What?

"Silas saw the two of you in the courtyard. He told me Kade forced himself on you."

Well, I didn't know he would kiss me, but if Silas had stayed he would have seen how after I got over the initial shock, I kissed Kade back. At least he hadn't found out about Tiernan yet.

"Well, I didn't *ask* him exactly, but I guess I sort of gave him permission to. It was for... training purposes."

Alaric narrowed his gaze at me, "Training purposes? Is that so?" He directed his question at Kade, who was now back to his usual, mischievous self, taunting Alaric with a 'come and get me' stare.

Kade shrugged, "Well, I mean, that was one purpose, I suppose, but I think she rather enjoyed it. Didn't you, Liana?"

Alaric growled, his chest expanding and hands balling to white-knuckled fists.

"Enough!" I yelled, jabbing a finger into Alaric's broad chest, "It doesn't matter who I kiss or don't kiss. That is at the very *bottom* of the list of things we should be worried about."

"Everything alright out there?" I heard Finn call from inside my chambers, offering me an escape and some separation from the territorial males who each seemed bent on having me all to themselves.

"For the record," I said sweetly, "You are all *mine*. And if you would stop trying to claim me as your own, I would allow myself to be yours too. *All* of yours."

Let that settle in their minds.

I meant it. I cared for all of them. And if I was being honest with myself, I *wanted* all of them. We were a team, and teams worked together, each member offering something different, yet vital.

Together, my warriors were stronger—and I would never choose just one to share myself with. It would be all or nothing.

And I wasn't even considering *nothing* as an option.

CHAPTER NINETEEN

*T*he days passed in a blur of training—which yielded no results, frustrating me to the point of giving up. The worst part was not knowing whether anything would *ever* come of it. Aside from the ability to *sort-of* withstand Kade's molten touch, I seemed to have no other talent.

Thana tried to coax the Grace of air from me, and Finn, the Grace of Ice. Alaric even tried to show me how to use the ability to control emotion in another even though he was stone-faced and sour as an underripe apple about the whole ordeal.

I had put it to him to decide how to proceed regarding our little situation. I made it clear I cared for each of the males and he wouldn't force me to choose. If he tried to make me choose, I would have none. He told me it wasn't the *sharing* that bothered him, or at least, that wasn't the only issue. It was how it would affect him and the others that worried him.

He worried they wouldn't be able to focus on their duty if they crossed that line. It could cause them to be distracted or cause them to react irrationally in situations. Someone could get hurt—or killed. But it was agony seeing them and being near them day in and day out—wanting to touch them, and wanting them to touch me, but none of us being able to until Alaric made the final decision.

A distraction, indeed. Though I thought *not* giving in would be an even greater distraction than to allow them to be satisfied. I couldn't explain the bond I felt between us. Even Finn, in these last few days had come around, spending the evenings guarding me as I slept in place of Alaric. There was a quiet energy about him I couldn't describe as if he had a hard outer shell shielding something worth discovering below the surface.

"You're so quiet," I said to Finn as I readied myself for bed, earning myself an inquisitive stare.

Finn shuffled his feet where he stood against the far wall of my bedchamber, "What would you have me say?"

I couldn't get the pin out of my hair, Thana had it so tangled in there I was sure I would need to cut it out. I tugged on it again, groaning, "I don't know, just *something*. Distract me from —" I grimaced, tearing at the pin with both hands now, "From all—well everything."

Finn strolled over to where I sat at my dressing table, catching my hand in his and removing it from my hair, "Stop that, you'll hurt yourself. Here," he said, deftly untangling and removing the pin within seconds. He straightened the mussed hairs back into place, running his fingers down their lengths to smooth them. "That's better."

"Do you think I'm crazy?"

"Crazy? No. Impulsive... definitely."

We shared a short laugh, and then Finn went back to his self-designated spot against the far wall after turning all the lanterns down low.

"Goodnight, Liana," he whispered through the dim, "Sleep well."

"'Night."

I crawled into bed and stared at the gossamer fabric woven like a canopy over my bed. *Sleep well...* I hadn't slept well in days. Finn had found nothing in the royal archives to help us and had returned to searching the scrolls of the library, where Tiernan had offered to help him. After I explained to Finn that Tiernan knew of the situation—and I trusted him, he begrudgingly accepted the emissary's help.

Nothing had come of monitoring Selbi *or* Edris. And the nobles were growing restless, wanting to know why their queen spent most of her time away from regular court functions. Everything was hanging in the balance, and it hinged on my being able to produce a Grace—which was something, it seemed, I couldn't do.

I thought I was drifting off when a murderous screech filled my bedchambers. I shot upright, bolting from the bed. Finn appeared in front of me, holding me back with one arm, brandishing a long sword in the other.

"What was that?" I whispered, trying to look out onto the terrace. Tiernan's falcon darted past.

Finn relaxed, lowering his sword, "That damned bird!" He stomped onto the terrace, leaning out to peer into the night. I caught his intake of breath before a shadow passed over the moon and something yanked him over the balcony.

"Finn!" I raced outside. Tiernan's falcon screeched again, but there was no sign of my sentry. "Finn!" I called again, pulse pounding in my ears.

The shadow shot up from far below, a winged male dressed all in black. A Draconian. He hovered in front of the terrace, not twenty paces from where I stood. His face was cast in shadow, but I could see his glowing eyes—the way they shone with the promise of destruction. He lunged for me and I fell back, landing hard on my tailbone.

His hands reached for me like talons—black hair blowing in the wind. He was knocked from reaching me by Finn, who had come soaring in from the abyss of black below. The two fought without weapons. The male with the black hair was fast, too fast for Finn to react, sending a bolt of lightning from his raised hands into Finn's chest. He fell, tumbling through the air, unconscious. "No!"

Hot tears welled in my eyes. I was half blind with them when the male dragged me from the terrace and shot into the sky. I writhed in his grasp, twisting and punching and kicking. I'd have preferred to die from the fall then be carried off to gods-knew-where with the winged beast. The palace grew ever smaller as the male carried me northward, towards the Wastes.

I heard Kade before I saw him, his growl pierced air. He shot skywards like a knife slicing up through the night. The male faked to the right, but Kade was ready, sword in hand. He sliced into the Draconian's wing, and the male cried out. He dropped me.

The ground rushed up to meet me in a blur of tree and rock. I threw my hands out, as though by sheer force of will alone, I could stop myself from falling.

"Kade!" I called, my voice muffled by the rushing wind.

A strong arm wrapped around my middle, lifting me into thick, warm arms. My breath came in ragged gasps. My vision blurred. I thought I saw the retreating form of the other male, his flight sloppy, falling and rising only to fall ever lower as he escaped.

"You're alright," he sighed through panting breaths, "You're alright."

"Finn," I choked out, "You have to find Finn."

Kade's arms tensed around me, his breathing stopping entirely. "Where—"

I grabbed his arm to steady myself and felt the heat fade from his skin, "He fell. He—he wasn't conscious. There, near the bay." I pointed to where he had fallen and could only prey he'd hit water and not land.

Kade sped toward the bay, tucking me in tight to his body,

and hurtled us as fast as he could. He spread his wings wide, stopping us to scan the cliffs and white-capped waves below.

I didn't see him at first, his limp form smashing against the cliffside with each strong thrust of the sea.

"Kade! There!"

He swooped us low, and a wave smashed Finn into the jagged rock again then pulled him out with the current. I spun in Kade's grip, "Lower!" I shouted at him over the roaring of the water.

Another wave shoved Finn into the rock again, splashing us with biting cold. A blue light streaked through the water, then another. *Wraiths.*

"Ready," Kade hollered, and when the current went back out, he dropped us, "Now!" he said, and the wraiths rushed to the surface, pushing Finn upwards. I wrapped my arms around Finn's middle, securing my hands together at his back, under his hanging wings. I searched the darkened waves, but the wraiths had vanished, back into the depths far below.

Kade buckled under the extra weight, his skin heating to that of a roaring fire. His heart pounded against my back, and his breaths came hot and fast against my neck.

"Finn," I said, searching his pale face for some sign of life. He was *heavy.* I wasn't sure how long I could hold on to him. "Kade, hurry!"

With a forceful roar, Kade lifted us to the top of the cliff, collapsing under the strain the moment we cleared the edge. We struck the ground. Fractals of light spotted my vision and a searing pain lanced through my ribcage.

I forced myself up, crawling to where Finn lay, sprawled on his back.

"Finn!" I screamed, my voice breaking. I grabbed him by his leather vest, shaking him. Was he breathing? I couldn't tell. His skin, it was so cold, like ice. Like he froze himself with his own Grace. *No.*

Kade lunged for his twin, "Step back, Liana," he ordered, and I obeyed, flinging myself backward onto the rock. He placed his hand on Finn's chest, eyes shining yellow. Steam rose from the Draconian warrior as he poured heat into his brother's limp form.

Finn stirred, and I gasped, my heart leaping. Kade then brought his hands up, clasping them together, and crashed them down into the centre of Finn's chest.

He convulsed, his body throwing itself into a seated position. He spewed water from his mouth. Choking. Shaking. I scrambled forward, wrapping my arms around him.

It took a moment, but Finn came back to himself, placing a hand on my back—holding me to him.

Kade blew out a long breath ending in a relieved laugh, "Welcome back, brother."

CHAPTER TWENTY

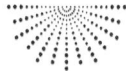

"*I*t isn't safe here," Alaric said, pacing the parlour. Against my wishes, he had forced the healer to work on me first before tending to Finn, who was recovering in my bed. "We need to leave."

Leave? "And give them what they want? Give up?"

Alaric turned on me with a mixture of wrath and despair in his eyes, "You were almost *taken*. And Finn nearly died. I'd rather see you *live* than see you keep your godsforsaken crown only to watch you die," he snarled through gritted teeth.

I crossed my arms over my chest, only then taking notice of my still damp night clothes, the white fabric transparent from the wet. He was right, and if Tiernan's Falcon hadn't warned us and then flew back to his master to awaken him, Tiernan wouldn't have found Kade in time to tell him something was wrong—and I'd be gone. And Finn would be dead. But... "I'll not run away like a coward."

"We're wasting time," Kade shouted, rising from his seat, "The Draconian was injured, he couldn't have got far. We need to find him."

Alaric threw his hands in the air, "*Go then*, but be back here before dawn."

Kade stood, and I stood to stop him, a hand wrapped around his bicep. I had wanted to ask him if he'd seen the wraiths in the water and if he knew why they would help us when only weeks ago, they'd tried to drown me, but that was a conversation for another time. "Be careful," I implored him. "The Draconian, he had a Grace I'd never seen before. He held lightning in the palms of his hands. He was strong."

"I'm stronger," he said, covering my hand with his own for but a moment before he left.

Alaric came to my side and watched Kade soar off into the distance until he was little more than a speck. "I vowed to protect you, Liana," he whispered, pain underlining each of his words, "And whether you're queen or not, I will uphold that vow. And so will they."

I leaned into him, and he wrapped an arm around my waist, resting his head atop mine, "I won't press you to flee, but I'm *asking* you to consider it. We could return... once you've developed your Grace and take back what belongs to you."

I had considered it. The answer was no. If the person who intended to take the throne had hired the Fae who worked to assassinate me, what sort of hands would I be leaving my court in?

At that moment Thana burst into the room. There would be no hiding this incident, it seemed. The servants had loose lips, and the walls did indeed have ears.

"Thank the gods," she exclaimed, rushing over to wrap me in a smothering embrace. My fractured ribs screamed in protest, but I bore the pain in silence. The healer could only do so much to repair them without depleting her Grace. Finn needed it more than I did. His kneecap was shattered, and his body bruised beyond recognition. The healer would remain throughout the rest of the night as I had ordered her to, using every ounce of her Grace until it fully recovered Finn.

"Thana, I'm alright, stop fussing."

She pulled away from me, turning to Alaric, "Where are the other sentries?" she asked him.

"Kade went to find the Draconian who tried to take Liana. And Finn is recovering."

"He's alive?"

Alaric's jaw tightened, "Yes."

It was then I noticed Thana was fully dressed, her hair wound in a sleek knot at the base of her skull—not in her night clothes as she would have been if she'd only just awoken. "Where were you?" I asked her, unable to help myself.

Her lips parted, closed, and then parted again, "I was in my chambers," she drawled, "I can't believe I didn't hear all the commotion when the attack happened. I must've been sound asleep," she finished in a rush.

I wanted to believe her, truly, I did—but Thana was a terrible liar, and had a habit of talking alternatingly slow and then fast when she told a false truth. I said no more, keeping the observation to myself. She deserved her privacy as much as anyone.

"I'm going to go be with Finn," I told Thana and Alaric, tired and confused and frustrated, wanting nothing more than to be alone with my thoughts, "Come and get me when Kade returns."

CHAPTER TWENTY-ONE

*K*ade didn't return until well after sunrise, but by
then, Alaric was too relieved to see him swoop
down onto the terrace to be angry. But I wasn't, "He said be
back before dawn, you inconsiderate oaf!" I had been staring at
the terrace for hours, wringing the hem of my shirt until the
threads frayed. I shoved him in the chest, hard, and he didn't
even have the decently to feign injury.

"Worried about me?" he asked with a cocky grin I'd have
liked to slap right off his smug face.

"Find him?" Alaric asked, but it was obvious he hadn't.

Kade shook his head, "I picked up his scent in the forest, but
I lost it near the foothills of the pass."

"The Wastes?"

"It's the only place he'd have been going."

Finn turned onto his side, wincing. He looked much better.
Most of the color had returned to his face, and the bruising had
faded. The healer needed to rest and replenish herself but
would be back to finish mending his knee when she awoke.
"There's nothing out there," Finn said, still groggy.

"That we know of," I said, and the three males shared a thoughtful look.

Alaric's eyes widened, "The Fae who have been going missing—their scents stopped at the same place, didn't it?"

Kade nodded, a grave shadow passing over his features.

"Send Jarrod and Quill to check it out," Alaric said to Kade with a dismissive wave of his hand. Jarrod and Quill were the other two sentries Alaric had chosen to join his retinue. I met them only for a moment before he sent them off to take over shadowing Edris and Selbi two days ago. Tiernan hadn't accepted my offer of a personal guard, and said he'd be alright on his own.

"Into the Wastes?"

"That's where the trail ended, isn't it?" Alaric retorted, stating the obvious. Kade clenched his jaw, muttering something about a waste of time, but left the way he came in to fulfill his captain's orders.

"I never thanked you," Finn said when I sat beside him on the bed. He had the covers pulled back, revealing his bare chest. Now free of bruises, the tan skin shone in the light of the rising sun, playing with the contours of his dormant muscle. "I don't know how you managed to pull me out of the water, but you did. I owe you a debt."

My eyes pricked at the sentiment in his voice, "You owe me nothing," I told him, wrapping my hand around one of his, still icy cold, but whether from the ordeal with the water, or from his Grace, I wasn't sure. "And it wasn't only me who saved you. Kade is the one you should thank, and the wraiths helped too."

"Wraiths?" Alaric asked, cocking his head, his brows pulled together. Finn held the same confused stare.

My lips pursed, "I don't understand it. They tried to drown me only weeks ago, but they were there last night, below the water. They pushed Finn into my arms. I may not have been able to grab hold of him if they hadn't helped. We owe them our thanks."

Finn blew out a breath, "I never liked those creatures. And I liked them even less when I heard about the incident you had at sea... But if you think I owe them my thanks, I'll give credit where its due. I'll leave them an offering." Wraiths were known to horde pearl and gemstones. It was said in their domain at the deepest part of the sea, was a treasure trove large enough to rival the one in my own palace.

I pulled a necklace of black pearl and silver from a long drawer in my dressing table and handed it to Finn. "Give them this," I told him.

He twirled the strand of pearls between his fingers, each one shining with deepest blue and purple when they caught the light just right. He chuckled, "I was thinking *one* pearl would be sufficient."

"Your life is worth more than all the pearls in this palace, Finn. It's a trinket. You know how I loathe jewelry, anyway."

Alaric stood at the foot of the bed, shaking his head, "Something doesn't add up. The wraiths wouldn't try to harm you and then *help* you."

He was right, and I remembered how they dragged me under the water and surrounded me. But they didn't hurt me, and they could've. I remembered their raspy song slicing through my oxygen-deprived mind. *Come with us*, they had said. But where they had wanted to take me, I wasn't sure.

"I'm not convinced they were trying to harm me," I told Alaric, trying to recall all the details of my encounter with the creatures. "They wanted me to come with them—I think."

"Go with them where?" Finn asked.

"I don't know."

CHAPTER TWENTY-TWO

*F*inn was back on his feet by mid-afternoon, with only a slight limp as proof of what had occurred the night before. He was the only one who agreed with me about thanking Tiernan for the role he played in helping us.

We found him in the library, intently reading a tattered scroll. "Your Majesty," he said, rising from his seat, "Are you well?"

"I am," I breathed, "Thanks to you."

Tiernan straightened his jacket, and I noticed he no longer wore the colors of his own court but was dressed in the traditional Night Court colors of deepest blue, white, and starlight silver. They suited him. "When Arrow woke me, I knew something was wrong. And then when I looked outside I saw Finn fall," he said, regarding the Draconian, "Glad to see you're both well."

"Arrow?"

"My falcon. He seems to be looking out for you," Tiernan said with a nod of his head to the bird now perched in the windowsill.

"Did you know Tiernan was a sentry in the Day Court's Royal Guard?" Finn asked me.

"You never told me that." I said to Tiernan. I had assumed like most nobles Graced with an earth-based ability he would've overseen the royal gardens or held a large parcel of land which could supply his court with wheat—or given his love for wine, perhaps grapes.

His lips curved up in a devious smile, "You never asked, majesty."

The information had my head filling with absurd ideas. A Day Court emissary, and previous protector of the Queen of Day, could never be part of my own Royal Guard, could they?

Don't be ridiculous, Liana. He wouldn't ever agree to that. He'd have to relinquish all ties to his home court for it to be possible. Maybe it was silly to even think such a thing. I'd only known him for little over a week... but in that time he'd shown strength, restraint, and had proved his trustworthiness. I could count the people I trusted at court on one hand, and Tiernan, whether or not he knew it, was one of them.

"Have you decided how long you'll be staying at court?"

He looked up at me through long lashes, his glinting green eyes flashing, "As long as you'll have me," he answered, his words taking on a double meaning, making my body quiver.

I met his fierce stare with one of my own, taking a steadying breath, "Then you may call me Liana from now on, as a friend would."

He licked his lips, and I felt Finn tense at my side, "Then I will endeavour to be your very *best* friend... Liana."

FINN and I arrived in my chambers that evening to find Kade sprawled on my settee, asleep. His top half resting on the cushion, and his legs dangling to floor. The settee no where near large enough to hold his full massive form.

Funny, he looked so innocent in sleep.

After the healer finished her work on Finn's knee and completed the healing on my ribs, he had escorted me around the palace. I stopped to talk to nobles, and other dignitaries, offering my sincere worry and condolences to Silas on the disappearance of his sister, and my wishes for her safe return.

Alaric—and Thana, thought it was of utmost importance to make myself present in the daily goings on of my court. To remind them I was their queen, and that I had no intentions of going anywhere. After hours spent placating nobles, and repeatedly lying about the great progress I was making in coaxing my Grace into developing, I was exhausted.

The stress was mounting, and if I had to see one more sour-faced noble, I would explode.

"Wake up," Finn chastised his brother, shoving him.

With a groan, Kade stretched out, his densely corded muscles flexing with the movement. He reached up to work a kink out of his neck, "What's wrong?" he asked me, his eyes squinting against the bright orange flare of sunset.

"Nothing," I replied, the frustration all but vanishing at the sight of an adorable, sleepy Kade. I snuggled onto the settee next to him and he wrapped an arm around me. I nuzzled into his neck, relishing in the soothing warmth and spicy scent I found there.

He hissed, "Careful, Liana. It's hard enough to contain myself *without* the feel of your breath on my neck."

Finn sat on the opposite side of me, his gaze faraway and his jaw clenched.

"What are you thinking?" I asked him in a whisper, reaching from the warmth of Kade to place a hand on his bare shoulder, shivering at the soft chill of his flesh.

He turned hostile eyes on me, but when he spoke, his voice was gentle, "You want him, don't you?"

"Want who?" I asked, not understanding his meaning.

Finn raised a dubious brow at me, "The emissary. I could smell the desire on you in the library."

I didn't know desire had a smell. But to someone who was part dragon, I supposed it could.

Kade tightened his arms around my waist, maneuvering his hips to press me into his groin. I gasped. "Is that so," he crooned, making my body tremble against him.

"No," I squeaked out, my voice taking on a husky tone.

Finn pulled my legs onto his lap, lazily stroking the skin around my ankles. I shivered. "Don't lie," he growled, and the sound reverberated in my chest.

Kade ground his hips, and I could feel the hardness of him against me. My breath came in hitched gasps, "A little competition never hurt anybody," the Draconian growled, lifting me in one swift motion. "But I never *lose.*"

He dropped me into the waiting arms of Finn, who pulled me into his chest. His words were a whisper against my neck, "Is this what you want?" he asked, his teeth grazing my neck, sending a ripple of pleasure coursing through me.

A moan tumbled from my lips, and Kade growled in response, kneeling before me on the carpet.

Finn's deft fingers stroked the sides of my bodice.

We can't do this. Alaric—something about Alaric... He would be angry... "Alaric—" I started, trying to shift away from Finn, but he gripped my waist tighter.

"*Alaric,*" Kade said through gritted teeth, "Only said we couldn't *have* you. He said nothing about touching you."

I watched as the Draconian licked his lips, his coal-black wings shivering, and his eyes glowing. He grasped the hem of my gown and reached a hand underneath to stroke the skin on the inside of my thigh.

I tipped my head back, my back arching at the wave of heat licking up my body. Finn swallowed my moan, claimed my mouth with his own. His kiss was all-consuming, filled with so much passion it settled over my heart with something more like pain. His hands on my waist tightened, gripping and releasing, strong. He tore the corset in half with one great pull, baring my breasts to the cool air. I felt his excitement in the hardening of his cock against my back.

He released my mouth, groaning at the sight of me. His hands cupped my breasts, fingers tracing wide circles around my nipples, the circles growing ever smaller until I couldn't stand the *need* pulsing through me with each hard beat of my pulse.

Kade's hand moved ever higher, until his knuckles grazed the dampened fabric of my undergarments. Those too were torn from me. Kade teased the skin around my sex, and my body convulsed. "You belong to us," he roared, "And no other."

I nodded vehemently, my hips trying to push against his hand—my body pleading, *no, begging* for release.

"Say it." Kade commanded, his index finger pressing against my opening.

Finn lightly flicked my nipple, and I heaved, "Yes," I managed, "I belong to you."

Kade plunged his fingers inside me, easing them in and out, his thumb circling the sensitive skin of my clit. He set a rhythm that had me on the cusp of release but slowed each time I was close to reaching it—teasing me. Finn groped my breasts, matching his twin's pace with each stroke, brushing my nipples with each pass of his rough hands.

My body writhed. Hips moving in tandem with each thrust of Kade's fingers. I was drunk with desire—aching with the innate need to find my release.

A whimper broke free from my chest, "Please," I urged them between pants, but Finn's lips came down on mine again, muffling my plea. His teeth skimmed my lower lip and stars danced along the edges of my vision.

Kade pushed harder, deeper inside me. Faster. And then

faster still. His touch heating as he activated his Grace. The inferno coiled up from within me. My head fell back, and I cried out. My entire body tightened. The flash of ecstasy tore through me, my every cell screaming yes, *yes*—as I finally fell over the edge.

CHAPTER TWENTY-THREE

*M*y sleep was deep and dreamless that night, the best I'd had since leaving the Isle of Mist. The path of the sun told me it was long past morning, and I sighed, sinking deeper into the covers.

"About time you woke up," Kade said, grinning from ear to ear, jumping onto the bed, "Thought we might've done some irreparable damage."

Oh, you did damage alright... I could still feel the ghost of their hands, and my stomach tightened at the memory.

"Stop biting your lip," Finn said, eyes darkening, "Or I'll ruin your nightclothes too."

"What did you just say?" Alaric asked Finn, entering my bedchamber without knocking, as usual.

Finn schooled his face into a look of professional indifference, "Nothing." He said plainly.

"Better be nothing."

Since the two Draconian's had been with me all night, I supposed it was Alaric who would guard me through the day. The feeling of disappointment surprised me. Only days ago, I wanted to spend all my time with him, now the sight of him frustrated me to no end.

"That's our cue," Kade said, launching himself from the bed, but not before giving me a wink and one of his trademark grins, "See you tonight."

Finn followed his brother from the room, cutting a sly glance my way before he closed the door behind them.

Alaric ran a hand through his hair, "They're setting up the table for lunch," he said, never once meeting my eyes, "Are you hungry?"

Once I thought about it, I was ravenous—and couldn't remember the last time I'd eaten a proper meal. I nodded, stepping from the bed to gather the airy lavender gown someone had set out next to the dressing table. A thought crossed my mind, and a sneaky grin tugged at my lips.

I stripped off my night clothes, letting them fall into a pile around my ankles. I delighted in the sound of Alaric's sharp intake of breath. If he wouldn't agree to what I had offered him —and his sentries, then he would be made to see what he was missing. With my eyes downcast, I took my time dressing, with slow, purposeful movements.

Once I had finished, pulling on a pair of sand-colored heels, I peeked up at him from beneath my lashes.

His eyes met mine, and I could see the beast in him, longing to be free. His hands twitched at his side, "So cruel," he breathed.

"I don't know what you mean," I replied sweetly, leaving the room with a shrug, the fabric of my skirt swirling around my legs.

Lunch was laid out on the table, a simple meal of breads, preserved meats, fruits, and various cheeses. But was that Nispero jelly? I hadn't had the fruit in years. It was my favorite, and only grew in the far south, and could only be harvested once per year. I lifted the spoon from the dish, reaching for a slice of bread. Alaric snatched it from my hand, clucking his tongue in disapproval.

Right. Selbi stood near the wall, waiting for me to sit before she began her tasting.

Alaric pulled my chair out for me, and begrudgingly, I dropped the spoon back into the pot and sat down. My stomach growled in protest.

She began her tasting and I could barely contain myself, my knees bobbing beneath the table.

"I've never seen someone get so excited about jam," Alaric teased.

I resisted the urge to snicker at him.

"Not just any jam," Thana said, entering from the parlour, "It's her favorite," she said and scooped a spoonful from the pot, slathering a piece of bread with glistening orange fruit. Selbi had already tasted it, but I had to wait until Rin came through and did the second tasting. I opened my mouth to warn Thana not to eat it but could say nothing in front of Selbi. Alaric seemed not to notice.

Thana bit into the bread, and I glared at her, "It's perfect," she said, and then wandered into my chambers, emerging a moment later with my crown. "I'm taking it to be polished, for the Solstice Ball," she announced before sauntering out of the royal quarters.

The moment Selbi left through the servants' entrance on the far side of the room, Rin came in through the main entrance, escorted by Tiernan. *Tiernan?*

"What are you doing here?" I asked him, looking at Alaric for the answer, and back to Tiernan when my captain didn't offer one.

"I offered to help. Kade and Finn needed rest, and I had nothing better to do."

"And the guards at his cell just *gave* him to you?"

Alaric cleared his throat, "I gave Tiernan permission to retrieve him."

"Why?"

Alaric leaned over me, splaying his fingers on the table, "Since you seem bent on keeping the emissary around—I thought he might as well be useful. Or do you have a problem with that?"

I didn't believe him. Not for a second. He didn't trust Tiernan, and likely never would. He had another motive, but I couldn't fathom what it was. "No," I told him, "I don't."

"Of course, you don't." Disappointment flared on his face before he turned back to Rin and Tiernan, "Rin, you may start."

Tiernan made himself scarce, standing with his hands clasped behind his back near the window. The breeze tugged at his golden hair, and the hazy sunlight painted his skin bronze. *Stop it, Liana.* An image of Kade came unbidden into my mind, kneeled before me, teasing me, torturing me, making me say I belonged to them as surely as they belonged to me. My skin bristled.

"Rin," Alaric said, drawing my attention back to the boy who clutched a spoon in his claw-like grip. A drop of golden jam dropped to the floor from its tip. Rin's eyes rolled into the back of his head, and my skin chilled. His head twitched back and forth violently. He lost balance and fell—Alaric catching him before he could hit the ground. As quickly as the poison took him, it released him, and I watched his body grow limp in Alaric's arms.

Rushing over, I called for a servant to fetch help and dropped to my knees in front of Alaric. He pressed two fingers to the boy's throat and listened at his mouth for breathing. "He's still alive," he said.

"Thana!" I exclaimed, "She ate it too."

"I'll find her," Tiernan said, his face drained of all color, and made for the door.

I jumped to my feet, "I'm going with you."

"No, you are not!" Alaric shouted, laying the boy down on the rug, "Wake Kade and Finn," he ordered the emissary, and then with a growl, "And bring me the taster. She *will* answer for this."

Of course. How could I not have realized... Selbi wasn't poisoned, which had to mean she was the one who poisoned the pot of jam. How did I not see her do it? *When* had she done it? I sent a silent prayer to the Gods that it was after Thana had already taken a bite.

CHAPTER TWENTY-FOUR

*T*he boy was still unconscious—his breathing shallow. The healer worked to ebb the poison's hold on him, and the apothecary worked to discern the type of poison used.

"It isn't verbane," the apothecary said, biting the inside of his cheek, "It's hawthorn ash, and not enough to kill—only enough to incapacitate."

The healer removed her hands from Rin at the words, "If it's hawthorn there's not much I can do. He'll awaken on his own when the effects wear off."

Hawthorn was toxic to Fae, and there weren't many of the trees left on the continent because of it. Even to a Fae-born mortal, the tree could cause harm.

"Thank you," I nodded to them both, "You may go. And please, tell no one of what you've seen here."

"Yes, majesty."

"Of course."

Once they were out of the room, Alaric, who was staring intently out into the day with a hand curled around the hilt of his sword turned to me, "See," he said, "Thana will be fine. Nothing to worry your pretty head about."

I crossed my arms over my chest, staring down at the paled and vacant face of Rin, "She had better be."

Moments later, Tiernan re-entered the room. Kade and Finn followed with a trembling Selbi in tow. Finn released her, and Kade shoved her into a chair, sniveling. My warriors came to me, Finn took my face into his hands, and Kade laid an uncharacteristically gentle hand on my shoulder.

"Are you hurt?" Finn asked me, releasing me when I shook my head.

I turned to Tiernan, who had busied himself inspecting the pot of jam, "Thana?"

He shook his head, "I'm sorry, Liana, I couldn't find her. The servants said they saw her recently, though, and told her what happened, so I'd expect she'll be on her way soon."

I nodded my thanks to Tiernan. At least Thana was alright, which meant Selbi hadn't dropped the hawthorn ash into the pot until after Thana had already eaten it.

"Is he dead?" Kade asked Alaric, gesturing to Rin, who was still lying on the floor.

Selbi sobbed quietly from her chair, her head in her hands.

Alaric left his post at the window, moving through the room with steady strides, "No, he will live. It was hawthorn, only enough to incapacitate." He stopped in front of Selbi and the taster flinched at his proximity.

"Where did you get the poison?" he asked her, and the calm with which he spoke was worse than if he had yelled.

Selbi raised her head, her shoulder-length hair parting like a curtain to reveal the fear in her deep brown eyes, "I—I didn't do this," she pleaded.

Alaric bent over, bracing his hands on his knees to get himself to eye-level with my taster, "I will ask once more, and if you lie to me again, there will be consequences. Now, where did you get the poison? Who gave it to you?"

"I said I didn't do this!" She shouted, her voice breaking near the end.

Alaric straightened to his full height, "Finn, take Liana to her chambers, she doesn't need to see this."

"No!" I yelped as Finn placed a hand on my lower back to guide me from the room, "I'll stay. I want to hear it myself."

"Kade," Alaric commanded, and the fire-Graced Draconian grabbed one of Selbi's wrists, a dangerous gleam in his eyes.

"Last chance," Kade said to Selbi, and she whimpered, trying to pull her wrist from my sentry, but he was too strong.

Her scream ricocheted through the dining room, the sound sharp enough to hurt my ears. My stomach tuned at the sound, and I swallowed back bile at the smell of burning flesh. Kade never released her wrist, but her screams eventually faded back to sobbing.

"I poisoned the queen," she said, her body shaking, "But I didn't do *this*. I swear. I—I took his money and—and I put the verbane in her wine like he asked, that's all."

Alaric and I shared a look at the mention of *he*.

Rustling up my courage, I knelt beside Selbi, "Who?" I asked her.

She cried in earnest then, "He'll kill me."

"I need you to tell me, Selbi."

Kade's grip tightened on her burned wrist, "Ronan," she hissed and Kade relaxed his grip, "Ronan gave me the poison, and told me to slip it into your wine," she said in a rush, "But—but when it didn't work, I told him I wouldn't do it again. He—well he said it didn't matter because you would never keep your crown."

My jaw clenched, and Alaric looked towards the entry with a murderous stare, as though he could will Ronan to appear—so he could rip him to shreds. I couldn't say it surprised me it was him, in fact, once I thought about it, he seemed the obvious candidate. I had stripped him of his position as Captain of the Royal Guard. This was his attempt at revenge.

Kade let Selbi's arm go, and she held it close to her chest, careful not to touch the ring of charred skin, "I don't even *have* any more verbane," she mewled, "I didn't do this."

I believed her. She wouldn't admit to one crime and not another, especially when one was enough to see her hung from the gallows. And it was hawthorn, not verbane used in this case. Though that didn't explain why she wasn't poisoned too.

The only other person who touched the jam pot was Thana. Alaric looked at me with a pained expression on his face, and I hated him for what I knew he was about to say, "Go find Thana," he told Kade and Finn.

The two Draconians exchanged confused looks, "What for?" Finn asked.

Alaric took a deep, shaking breath, "Just find her... and send Silas up here. His sentries will have to arrest Ronan. If I see the bastard, I'll rip his fucking head off."

"It's not her," I told Alaric once the others had gone—Kade and Finn to find my handmaiden, Selbi, escorted by Tiernan to the dungeons, and Rin, carried to the infirmary by the servants. "It's impossible. She's been with me since birth, Alaric," and then I added in terms he would understand, "If she had wanted me dead, I'd be buried on the isle."

Ronan, on the other hand, *had* wanted me dead.

Silas was in a state of shock, outraged at the discovery that someone on the council would attempt to assassinate a descendant of Morgana. Though, he admitted, he'd never like the bastard, and would be happy to see him hang for his crimes. He left to gather a few sentries to aid in helping him apprehend the former captain. I knew Ronan wouldn't go quietly and was immediately exhausted at the idea of announcing his betrayal to my court.

"I know," he said, his jaw taut as he raked a hand through his hair, "I don't want to think she's to blame either, but it's the only plausible explanation."

"It's ridiculous."

Finn and Kade returned, "She was poisoned," they said together. "We found her near the gardens, unconscious. She's in the infirmary with Rin, but she'll wake," Finn added.

"What do you have to say now?" I asked Alaric, rising from the settee, "You were wrong," I added before he could answer.

He nodded, "That doesn't explain how she could make it all the way down to the gardens before the poison took its effect. And why Tiernan wasn't able to find her earlier."

"So, she poisoned herself, then? Is that what you're saying?" I asked him, incredulous, unable to contain the rolling of my eyes, "*Just stop*, Alaric. Thana had nothing to do with this."

"Whoever is responsible, they wanted you incapacitated, but not dead. And the Draconian who attacked us the other night could have killed you but didn't. If Ronan is the one behind these attacks, then you could be safe now he's been imprisoned... but if it isn't Ronan, or if he's working with someone else, the threat remains," Finn said—the first sensible thing I'd heard in hours.

"What do we do?" I asked, posing the question to no one in particular. Finn had only just recovered from the attack not two moons past, and I shuddered to think what would happen if the Draconian returned to finish what he started... or what could happen if there were more than one of them this time.

"We take you someplace safe," Alaric said, raising a hand to silence me when I opened my mouth to protest, "Only until we've sorted this out. A couple of days, at most. I promise. One of us will remain at the palace at all times. And if anyone asks, you are in your chambers, preparing for the Solstice Ball. It will be as though you never left."

I couldn't argue with him. It wasn't only about me anymore. It was their duty to keep me safe, but it was my duty not to forcibly put them into harms way. I wouldn't have any of them hurt because I stubbornly refused to go when all the signs pointed toward danger if I stayed.

"Very well," I agreed, wringing my hands in the fabric of my gown. "A couple of days, and no more." Excuses for my absence would only hold out for so long.

CHAPTER TWENTY-FIVE

$\mathcal{W}$e left the palace under cover of darkness. The four of us took to the skies, me in the arms of Finn, and Alaric carried by Kade and looking wholly undignified. It would have been too simple for anyone to track us had we gone on foot.

They described the place where we headed as modest, but secluded—and secluded was what we needed.

They told Tiernan nothing—against my better judgement, but Alaric said he couldn't risk anyone knowing where we were going, or even that we'd left at all.

Finn adjusted me in his arms, tucking my legs around his waist. "Comfortable?" he asked me, wrapping his arms around my middle. I was glad I'd accepted Alaric's cloak before we left, even with it, the chill of the night was almost enough to set my teeth chattering. At least in that position, tucked close to Finn's expansive chest, we could share body heat, and I sighed at the warmth as it seeped into my skin.

"Much better," I crooned, nuzzling my cold nose against the bare skin above his vest.

He pressed me tighter into him, planting a soft kiss in my hair, "We're almost there, look," he whispered.

I turned but saw nothing that looked like a homestead. We were miles away from the palace now, having flown for nearly an hour. We passed the last sleepy village a while back. Since then it had been nothing but forest.

We were nearing the shoreline on the eastern edge of Meloran—so much different from the western side's tall cliffs and rocky terrain. The forest broke way to sandy beaches that seemed to sparkle in the moonlight. Waves gently lapped at the shore, and there, squatting in a copse of trees near the water, stood a cottage.

It was small, no more than the size of my parlour back at the palace. Moss covered its thatched roof, which looked to be in need of repair. The structure beneath was made of stone brick, and the mortar looked like it had seen better days. We dropped to the ground in front of the door, and I nearly tripped when Finn lowered my feet to the earth, off balance from the long flight.

"It belonged to my mother," Alaric said, leading us inside, "No one else knows where it is. You should be safe here."

The interior was pleasantly surprising, and larger than it looked from above.

Kade lit a fire in the hearth—the task taking him seconds—bathing the room in an orange glow. It was an open space, with a sitting area, a small kitchen, and a long settee pushed close to the fireplace. There were two other rooms, one to the right and left, which meant one had to be a bathing room, and the other, a bedchamber.

I fell onto the settee, a plume of dust rising around me, and leaned in to feel the warmth of the fire.

Kade came to sit next to me, and tugged me onto his lap, "You're like a damned icicle," he exclaimed, "Finn, you idiot, you should've said something. We could have traded."

"I'm fin—" I started, but then Kade used his Grace to warm me and I quivered in delight, a sound somewhere between a sigh and a moan sliding out.

"There you go," Kade said, and tucked one of his hands under my rear, making me gasp at the instant relief from the cold—and the primal desire he was awakening between my legs.

"One of us has to go back," Finn said from somewhere behind us, "Question Ronan."

"Kade," Alaric said, "You'll head back first, and when you return, I'll go with Finn and you'll stay here with Liana."

"Does he have to leave right now?" I whined, pulling him tighter against me to make the warmth last longer.

Kade laughed, his ochre eyes glinting in the firelight, "I should." He disentangled himself from me, giving my rear a playful squeeze, "You're all mine tomorrow," he whispered in my ear before he stood. My stomach flipped at the promise in his words.

"I heard that," Alaric scolded, but said nothing more to his sentry before Kade was back out the door, wings spread, soaring back the way we'd come.

"Try again," Finn said, popping a few more berries into his mouth, "Think cold thoughts."

But the water stayed water, no matter how hard I tried to turn it to ice. "This is pointless," I stated, beyond frustrated. It was late morning, and we had been at it since dawn. It was Alaric's suggestion I used the time we had in seclusion to coax my Grace into emerging without the prying eyes at court. "I can't do it."

"Not with that attitude," Alaric said, entering the cottage with two rabbits hanging limp from his fist. He set to cleaning the animals, getting a pot of water to boil over the fire. Seeing him do such a mundane task was strange and made me wonder what his life was like before he enlisted in the Horde armies, and before I threw him to the wolves at court.

Finn moved behind me, and rubbed the ache out of my shoulders, "Try one more time, if it doesn't work, we'll try something else."

It was hard to focus with Finn's hands kneading me into a trance, but I tried setting my hands back down on the table next to the clay bowl. I took a deep breath and pulled from within my core, picturing a force like a great ever-spinning ball of ice like Finn told me to.

My chest grew cold, and an electrifying energy sped through my veins, my back arched at the release of power and my eyes flew open. Frost blossomed from my palms, freezing the table— spreading up onto the clay bowl. I pushed harder, forcing the ice from my body. The bowl shattered under the immense cold and water flooded the table. Finn jumped back, and I pulled my hands away, breaking out of the trancelike state.

"You did it," Alaric exclaimed, rushing over to lift me from the ground in a crushing embrace. "Ice. Your Grace is ice, Liana!"

Ice. I had finally done it. I was Graced. My ancestors *hadn't* abandoned me. Relief rushed through me, detangling all the tensed muscles the stress of not knowing had created.

Finn pulled me from Alaric to wrap me in an embrace of his own, though Alaric still held one of my hands. "Congrat—" The Draconian jumped back as though burned, dropping his arms. He stumbled back, bumping into the now thawing table.

"What did you just do?" he asked me, raising a hand to his chest, "I felt—it was like—"

Alaric cocked his head at my sentry, "What is it, Finn?"

But he simply shook his head, "Never mind, it was nothing," he said, and went back to eating his berries in pensive silence.

CHAPTER TWENTY-SIX

*N*o matter how hard I tried, I couldn't conjure the ice again. What good was a Grace if I couldn't use it when I wanted to? Alaric told me to give it more time, but Finn seemed confused and told me even when he was still developing his Grace, he could at least summon a bit of frost.

Alaric spoke to Kade in private when he returned, but I got the gist of their conversation, overheard in snippets and chunks. Thana and Rin remained unconscious and Ronan offered nothing to explain the second attempt at poisoning me, nor the foreign Draconian's attack. Even though, by the sound of it Kade hadn't gone easy on him—burning one of his hands down to bare bone.

I knew it was ridiculous to feel sorry for my former Captain —he had tried to kill me, but I saw the pain in Selbi's eyes when Kade used his Grace on her, and he had gone easy then. I couldn't imagine what the full force of his fire felt like and wouldn't wish it on anyone.

"But he admitted to giving Selbi the verbane?" Alaric asked Kade for the second time, their voices drifting into the sitting room.

"Yes."

"Good. Finn and I will try to get more information from him, but at the very least, that crime alone is enough to see him executed. At least one threat will be dealt with."

The two returned to the sitting room, and Alaric belted his sword to his waist, "We'll be back in the morning," he said by way of goodbye, brushing a strand of my hair behind my ear, "Be safe," he said. "Any sign of trouble and you run, understand?"

I nodded, though since we arrived I hadn't seen another soul, and there were no roads to be seen anywhere around the cottage. I didn't expect any visitors, welcome ones or no.

"So," Kade said after Finn and Alaric left, "Alaric told me your Grace is ice. And I've got to say, I'm not buying it."

I raised my brows at him, blowing air out my lips, "Is that so?"

"Yes, it is," he said, coming nearer. He was shirtless and the hourlong flight had further darkened his tan skin, making the ochre of his eyes seem brighter and his hair copperier than it had been before. He was magnificent, and I wished I could find a flaw on his body, if only to prove he was real, and not a figment of my imagination. "There's fire in you. I know it's there. I feel it calling to me when I touch you."

Regardless of what some old librarian told me about Morgana, I knew it was impossible to have more than one Grace. It had never happened. The only way to gain a second Grace was to steal it using the Blessed Blade, and that was a myth—a bedtime story used to scare children into listening to their elders.

"I'm bored," I said, changing the subject before he asked me to prove my Grace to him, because I wasn't sure I could. "I'm going for a swim." I told him and pulled a few laces free from my corset.

He growled at the subtle invitation and rushed to follow me

from the cottage. The gown and corset were off of me within seconds, and I shivered at the feel of the sun on my bare back. With only my sheer panties left to clothe me, I ran into the water, sucking in a tight breath when my skin met the cool sea.

I dove under and pushed myself out, swimming further, and further from the shore. When I came up for air, Kade was hopping on one foot, trying to pull off his other boot.

"Wait," he called over the waves, "Not too far."

I laughed and plunged under again, pushing past the breakwater and out into the calm blue. The sunlight shone through the surface of water, reflecting on the sandy floor in a wavy pattern of gold. I had missed this. I hadn't swum for weeks, and before I left the isle, it was something I did every day—if only to escape the lessons and constant ridicule of Thana.

The water was an old friend, welcoming me into her cool embrace. I came up for air only once, and pushed myself further, deeper, relishing in the burn of my muscles.

A shape darted near in my peripherals. A streak of shining sapphire. I spun and was face to face with a wraith. Bubbles of air exploded from my mouth as I tried to make for the surface. But it wrapped a tentacle around my ankle, holding me in place.

With light shining down through the water, the wraith was crystal clear, and I was awestruck at its dangerous beauty. Its upper half was humanlike, with breasts and a narrow waist, though its skin was a translucent blue that glowed from within. Six tentacles made up its lower extremities where legs would have been. But it was the wraith's face that drew me. Big eyes, black as ink seemed to stare *into* me. The eyes set in a small, angular heart shaped face, with perfect lips and a wild mane of silver hair, not unlike my own.

Hauntingly beautiful.

Not hurt you. Never hurt you. its raspy song-like voice wrapped around my mind, scraping at my skull.

You're hurting me right now! I wanted to shout at it, it's grip on my ankle was like a vise—any tighter and it would fracture the bone.

Must listen. It crooned, *not safe... Queen must not return to her stone tower. He will not stop. Queen will fall... Queen must stay here. Queen is safe here.*

My lungs were constricting. I needed air. I needed to get to the surface. The last of my breath was forcibly trickling from my mouth as I tried to pull the tentacle off me.

Let me go!

A dark shape hurtled towards us from behind the wraith, speeding through the water unlike anything I'd ever seen. His wings expanded, and contracted, pushing him faster toward me. *Kade.*

The wraith must've heard him coming. Without warning she released my ankle and pushed me upward to the surface before she disappeared quick as a loosed arrow out to sea.

The air hurried to fill my lungs when I broke the surface. I was light-headed and fought to stay afloat.

"Where'd it go?" Kade bellowed, bursting from the water not an arms length away. Steam rolled from his shoulders, and the water near me warmed as his anger unleashed his Grace. But the steam stopped, and the water cooled when he beheld my face, "Damn, Liana," he cursed, pulling me to him, "Lets get you back to shore."

CHAPTER TWENTY-SEVEN

*K*ade had me wrapped in a blanket on the settee. A fire blazed in the hearth.

"No shit you aren't safe at the palace," he said after I told him what the wraith said under the water, "We know that, already."

"But it said *he* will not stop. Do you think it was talking about Ronan?"

Kade handed me a mug of warm tea and sunk down onto the settee beside me, wearing nothing but his still damp trousers, "I don't know, Liana, but good intentions or not, if another one of those ugly things touches you, I'll kill it."

"You can be such a brute," I told him, earning myself a tight-lipped smirk from the Draconian. I shoved him, "I'm *fine*," I told him for the third time since he'd pulled me from the sea. "And I promise, no more swimming, ok?"

His ochre eyes fell on me, tracing a line from the top of my head down to my collarbone, stopping to rest on my exposed shoulder.

"It's getting late," he said, "You should get some rest. With any luck, Finn and Alaric will get to the bottom of these assassination attempts and we'll be back at court tomorrow."

I nodded but knew sleep wouldn't come, I was too wired on the aftereffects of the adrenaline still coursing through my body. Rising from the settee, I dropped the blanket to the floor, baring myself to the fire. My skin was still slick with wet from the sea but dried as I neared the hearth.

A low rumble started in Kade's chest, audible from where I stood—just out of his reach. "Liana," he warned, and I turned to find him clutching the arm of the settee. The look in his eyes made my insides squirm.

"Yes, Kade?" I said, knowing exactly what the sight of my near-naked body was doing to him. Etiquette be damned. After so many days spent in perpetual worry, I wanted to feel good —*needed* an escape, and I knew my golden-eyed warrior would oblige me.

Kade locked his lips onto mine before I had time to register he'd moved. The kiss was not gentle, it was wild and hard and hungry. His warm chest brushed against my breasts and my nipples hardened in response. His tongue flicked against mine and I moaned, my nails biting down into the hard muscle of his back.

"Gods, Liana," he said between fervent kisses, his hands exploring the curves of my hips, "I want you," he growled, and pressed his cock against me, compelling another moan from my lips. The feel of his hardened length made my pulse thunder in my ears. As if in answer to an unasked question, my sex wetted.

He lifted me onto him, his hands cupping my backside, and carried me to the bedchamber. I fell onto the bed, and he bent over me, his wings spreading out to reach either side of the room, surrounding us in a cocoon of tempered darkness.

I reached up to stroke the soft membrane, and his delicious groan reverberated in my core. He pinned my hands above my head and descended upon me. His tongue flicked my nipple and my back arched, breath coming in ragged gasps. He reached down with his free hand and my panties vanished with a flick of his fingers.

Kade moved slowly, like a wildcat stalking its prey, licking and nipping and biting flesh as his mouth went ever-lower. He released my hands and took hold of my hips with burning fingers, tugging me to the edge of the bed.

"What are you—" I said, but the words were swallowed up by the raw—pure sensation cascading through me when his mouth settled over my sex. His tongue circled my opening, and my body tightened in response. My hips moved against him, urging him to go faster, harder. I thought I might die from the building pressure—from the heat. From the unchecked energy coursing over me, through me.

The heat built to a precipice, and I bucked and writhed, calling out his name as my release exploded through me.

My eyes flew open and were met with fire. Where my hands had been clutching the cotton sheets a fire was spreading. Kade jumped back, pulling me from the bed. His hands felt cold against the blaze of my skin. He released me as though burned, and the fire in my palms extinguished.

I couldn't move—could hardly breathe. What had just happened? Kade darted to grab a pitcher of water from the basin and tossed it over the bed. A plume of smoke coiled up from the blackened, tattered bedding.

My Grace was ice—not fire. *I couldn't have...*

"I *knew* it," Kade said, "I knew your Grace was fire."

But only that morning, frost had blossomed beneath my fingers.

Impossible.

CHAPTER TWENTY-EIGHT

*T*hree days had passed since we first arrived at the cottage. They passed in a blur of mind-numbing lessons and constant arguments. If I had to stay another night, I felt I'd go mad.

My Grace, or *Graces* seemed only to present themselves when one of the twins was touching me. I could summon ice without issue when Finn laid a hand on my shoulder, and I could conjure fire with a flick of my finger when Kade did the same. But the moment they released me, I would lose all control over the abilities. It made no sense, and though Tiernan had been tirelessly searching the archives for more information, the males told me he had found nothing to explain it.

"The Solstice Ball is tomorrow night," I shouted in exasperation at Alaric. "I don't care if Ronan is to blame for all the attacks or not, I *must* return to court. I've been away too long already, and you said yourself, the nobles are starting to wonder. And Thana is probably sick with worry."

Alaric itched at the stubble on his jaw, lost in thought.

"Alaric!" I shouted louder to get his attention.

"Hmmm—oh… right. Yes, I know it's tomorrow. Darius brought your gown to your chambers last night before I left."

"So?" I asked, drawing out the word.

Alaric took another drink of his mulled wine, setting the empty goblet down onto the table, "We'll all stay here tonight," he declared, "Rest. And tomorrow at dawn we'll return to the palace."

I sighed in relief, eager to return to my bed, to see Thana and to present a Grace to my court, though I hadn't decided which one. It would have to be large enough of a spectacle that everyone could see. Kade suggested setting my gown on fire and letting it burn off me—*not surprising*. And Finn suggested turning the entire floor to ice and watching all the nobles fall on their backsides. The latter sounded more appealing than I cared to admit, but either way, one of the Draconian warriors would have to be in contact with me for me to do anything.

The lines on Alaric's beautiful face had deepened with worry over the last few days. And it pained me to see him that way even though I was still angry with him for more than one reason. I moved into the seat next to him, and pulled his hands into my lap, "Hey," I said, "It'll be alright. We'll figure this out. Together."

He gazed into my ever-changing eyes, his tensed shoulders relaxing, "I hope so."

"I know so," I said, giving his hands a tight squeeze. "I've been hard on you, but I know you're doing all you can to keep me safe. And—well I want to thank you."

I kissed him on the cheek and his lips tipped up into a sad smile before he rose and went into the bedchamber alone, closing the door behind him.

CHAPTER TWENTY-NINE

*W*e snuck onto the terrace of my bedchamber the next morning just before sunrise. Alaric sent Kade to meet the sentries he had sent to the Wastes. We saw them returning to the palace from the northern road as we flew overhead. And now Alaric was using my bathing room to get himself cleaned up—having refused to go back to his own quarters. Once finished, he would fetch Thana to ready me for the ball.

Finn leaned against the wall, studiously picking something from under his fingernails. He had been suspiciously quiet since returning to the cottage after I set the bed ablaze. I had an inkling I knew what he thought had happened, and though he wasn't far off, he was wrong. "Kade and I—" I began, "We didn't —well we didn't do what you think we did."

"It's not that, Liana. I'm worried about you is all. It isn't possible for Fae to have two Graces. One is enough to control. Kade nearly burned our entire village to the ground when he was learning to control his."

"I can't even access mine without help, so I doubt that will be an issue."

He sighed, readjusting his wings behind him, "Which makes this all even more confusing." He pushed off from the wall, and the stone splintered—the outline of a doorway materialized where he had stood.

A doorway?

I ran toward it, pulling on the edge of the clean-cut stone.

A passageway lay behind it, dark, and seeming to go on forever. Finn cursed from behind me, and took hold of my wrist, "Step back," he warned.

But the familiar pull in my chest began again—the same one that drew me towards the Great Hall all those nights ago. I was thinking I had imagined it.

Liana... the ominous voice called.

"Did you hear that?" I asked Finn, pulling my wrist out of his grasp.

"Hear what?"

"I'm going inside."

"No, you aren't." Finn said, stepping in front of me to block the passageway. "We have no idea where this leads. Go get Alaric."

Come... the voice said, and the pull in my chest intensified, becoming almost painful. I winced.

Alaric would only drag me from the palace again at the discovery of a hidden passageway leading right to my bedchamber. No, I wouldn't go get Alaric. The force expanded in my chest, and I curled inward, gasping.

I hated myself for what I was about to do, but I *had* to go inside. "I order you to step aside."

He was taken aback at the command, and the shock broke way to hurt as he looked away and stepped from my path. "I can't let you go in there alone," he said between gritted teeth.

"Then don't," I answered him, stepping into the shadows, "Grab a torch. We'll need it to light the way."

My chest tightened as we delved further into the gloom. The

torchlight illuminated the way as we followed the path down a flight of slippery stone steps. Bats clung to the rough ceiling, squeaking and writhing as we passed under them. Finn was careful not to disturb them, lest they attack.

The pull in my chest strengthened, propelling me to go faster, almost running through the dark.

Finn cursed, "Slow down," he said in a harsh whisper, "You'll slip."

It grew cold as we descended, down and down *and down*. For a time, it seemed there would be no end to the stairs, but then there was the sound of water, and we rushed to clear the last few steps.

The moment we entered the cavernous chamber, a hundred torches flared to life, ringing the walls in flickering blue flame. The chamber was empty save for a statue at the center. It was Morgana, standing tall with a look of defiance in her eyes. The water we heard ran from the palms of her outstretched hands, cascading over her fingertips and falling into a pool around her feet. Four dragons carved of the same stone formed a barrier around her, their faces shaped to portray a primal fury.

Liana... The voice said, sounding as though it was right next to my ear. I spun, but only Finn was there, staring in awe at the statues.

"What is this place?" he murmured, the question more for himself than for me.

He is coming...

"Who is coming?" I asked.

"Who are you talking to?" Finn asked me.

And I knew in that moment, the voice I heard in the chamber was Morgana.

His power is growing. He won't stop until he's reclaimed the throne.

"Who?"

My father, Morgana hissed.

The Mad King? "He's dead."

No, my child... The Mad King did not fall in the battle of Mount Noctis.

"Is he here? In the palace?"

A bolt of cold fear raced up my spine.

You must destroy him...

But how? I shook my head, unwilling to believe what I was hearing—that I was hearing her voice at all. Had I gone mad?

"Liana, come. Let's go back," Finn begged, tugging at my waist, a look of concern twisting his features.

You have my Graces... it now falls upon you to finish what I started.

So, it was true. Morgana had more than one Grace... and she had passed them on to me.

"I cannot wield them. I can't destroy anyone."

She did not answer—did not offer a solution. But the pull in my chest started again, drawing me to her statue—through the stone dragons. Finn followed me, his sword drawn as though he expected one to rise and attack us.

The trickle of water slowed and then stopped. On tip toe, I looked into her hands, finding a ring of purest silver, with a yellow gemstone at its centre. The gem was unlike any I owned, in the shape of a diamond with flecks of gold, amber and onyx throughout. It looked like a dragon's eye.

It's your burden to bare now, my child...

I lifted the ring, and settled it onto my middle finger, feeling it pulsate with some unknown force against my skin. I shivered, clutching my hand to my chest.

Never take it off.

A clatter had Finn and I spinning to face the entrance, but it was only Alaric, wide-eyed and breathing hard, his face red as the evening sun.

It took the better part of an hour to explain what had happened in the chamber belowground. They had too many questions I couldn't answer and grew frustrated at hearing the same response of 'I don't know,' after each one they asked.

"I believe what you're saying is true," Alaric told me, "As difficult as it is to believe... But what I need to know is if there is any truth to what this *voice* told you."

"It was Morgana. I know it was."

He raised his hands in a placating gesture, "We all know the Mad King is dead, Liana, and has been for two millennia."

I fell back onto my bed, pinching the bridge of my nose to attempt to stop my head from pounding, "I know."

A servant knocked on the door then, and as one, our three heads turned at the sound.

"Begging your pardon, majesty, but Thana has arrived."

The Solstice Ball was to begin in mere hours, and I still hadn't bathed. One glance in my dressing-table mirror and I knew combing the knots from my long silver hair would take an hour on its own.

"Send her in," Alaric told the servant when I neglected to say anything. "I'll stay with you while you get ready. Finn, you can go get yourself cleaned up. I doubt anyone will try anything in such a public place, but I'll need both you and Kade there just in case."

Finn nodded to his captain and left the room at the same time Thana entered, without so much as a goodbye. Guilt weighed upon my shoulders at what I had forced him into. *I should never have* ordered *him the way I did.*

"Where have you been?" Thana shrieked upon entering my bedchamber, "I've been worried to death."

"The queen had some matters to attend to away from court," Alaric offered as an excuse for my absence.

Thana's hands landed on her hips in a dramatic gesture, "Oh, you *speak* for her too now?" she said sarcastically.

I rose to wrap my handmaiden in an embrace and felt some

tension ease out of her limbs, "I'm sorry I had to leave while you were ill. Are you feeling better?"

She pursed her lips, pulling away, "I'm fine, child." She pulled my arm, spinning me in a circle before her, "But you are an absolute mess. This will take me hours to fix. Where did you have to go, a pig farm? You're filthy. And that hair—" she gasped, "You'll be lucky if I don't just cut it off to save us some time."

"You will do no such thing," I told her, "I quite like my long hair."

I reached up to comb out some tangles with my fingers, and Thana cocked her head at me, her face seeming to pale. "That ring," she said, pointing to the dragon's eye stone on my finger, "Where did you get it? It looks so familiar."

"It was—" I started but stopped when Alaric elbowed me in the ribs. I didn't like keeping secrets from Thana but did *not* feel like dealing with Alaric's wrath tonight. I would tell her the truth some other time—or show her the chamber beneath the palace. She would be in awe of the beautiful statues even if she couldn't hear the original queen's voice.

I showed her the ring closer, letting her get a better look, "Just a trinket," I told her, sighing.

She reached for it, but halted her hand a hairsbreadth away, "It's beautiful," she exhaled, shaking her head as though coming out of a daze, "And it'll look beautiful with your gown."

CHAPTER THIRTY

*T*hana was right of course; the gown Darius had designed for the ball was breathtaking. It was a deep crimson, beaded and trimmed with whorls of black and gold. Tight-fitted in the chest and around my waist, flaring out delicately at the hips to accentuate my curves. Another masterpiece. No surprise.

Thana had piled my hair at the nape of my neck—after what felt like hours of merciless brushing, leaving a few gently curling strands to hang near my face. She had ringed my eyes in feather-light line of coal, and a smattering of powered gold. Alaric watched the entire transformation from beginning to end, seeming to grow more uncomfortable as the minutes passed.

"What do you think?" I asked him, eager for a second opinion. Tonight, I would not only be rejoining my court from days spent absent but also revealing a Grace.

Alaric cleared his throat, clasping his hands together at his front, "Perfect, as always."

I beamed. "You clean up quite nicely too," I told him, winking over my shoulder at him. He had the servants bring up his clothes, and though he still wore black, as was customary for the Royal Guard, he had added a bit of flare. He wore a long gold-trimmed jacket over his vest which seemed to make his shoulders even broader and brought out the light in his eyes.

Thana had nothing but questions to throw at me as she readied me for the ball. When she had asked me if I had made any progress in developing my Grace, I had told her it was a surprise and I would show it to everyone later. She had smiled ear to ear and had demanded I tell her *immediately* what my Grace was. But I hadn't decided which to reveal and made her wait in pouting suspense like the rest of the nobles at court.

Eventually, I would tell her the truth.

WALKING into the ballroom was like walking into a living work of art. Golden draperies, tied with red sashes adorned every window. A fountain of ever-flowing sparkling wine occupied the far wall, and long tables laden with glistening fruits, dark chocolates and canapes were dispersed throughout the space. Every noble, even those from far-off towns and villages seemed to have made the journey. The females were dripping in gemstones and the males were dressed in expertly tailored jackets.

Though there was a more important reason for my attendance, I got lost in it all—wanting to taste from each platter, and drink until my mind numbed. A song of harp and lute cast an ethereal feel over the gathering.

I accepted greetings from the nobles in attendance and was sure to promise each of the announcement to be made later that eve. Spirits lifted even higher as news of my upcoming debut spread like wildfire through the room, and within minutes they regarded me with wide smiles and the lifting of fluted glasses.

Alaric and I had made it to the other side of the room when Kade and Finn entered from one of the many smaller entrances, scanning the assembly to find us. My feet froze in place at the sight of them—they were immaculate. Both wore snuggly fitted outfits in opposing shades of white and black. Black on Kade, and white for Finn. I'd never seen them in anything but their standard guard uniforms of vest and trousers.

As Finn turned, I could see their jackets had been custom-made, and had slits all the way up the back to accommodate their wings. Kade grinned when he saw me, gliding over with the swagger of a king.

He dropped to one knee, and kissed the back of my hand, allowing his lips to linger there a moment longer than would have been acceptable.

"You look ravenous," Kade said, his voice husky, licking his lips.

"I think what you meant to say is she looks *ravishing*," Alaric corrected.

Kade shook his head, never taking his eyes off me, "No. I meant what I said."

Finn strolled up a moment later, "Have you decided which Grace to present?" he asked, demure. I wondered how much longer he'd be upset with me. I could only apologize so many times. It was *painful* to ignore the call of Morgana. Her pull on me was near impossible to resist, but I didn't think he would understand that, even if I told him. Out of the three of them, though Finn was there, he seemed the most skeptical about what had in fact occurred in Morgana's hidden chamber.

"There she is!" Edris almost shouted, moving across the floor with a half-empty drink in his hand. He gave a slight bow, "Are the rumors I've been hearing true, majesty? Have you discovered the nature of your Grace?"

It was painstaking obvious my father had had too much to drink already even though the evening had only just begun. After shadowing the former King Consort, Alaric had discovered nothing to implicate him. What he learned was Edris urged the council to give me more time and had blatantly refused to assume the title of King if they succeeded in overthrowing me. I was wrong about him. *We* were wrong about him.

"It's true," I obliged him, "Though you'll have to wait like all the others to find out what it is."

"Of course."

Edris downed the remaining drops of his wine and dumped the empty glass on a servant's tray as she passed by, "I believe they're about to begin," he said, pointing to the musicians. The nobles moved to the walls, forming a hollow circle in the center of the floor, and couples paired off for the first dance of the eve.

Alaric must have noticed the look on my face at Edris' subtle invitation. He stepped in front of Edris and offered me his hand. "Can I have the first dance?"

I swallowed, giving Edris a tight-lipped smile and placed my hand into Alarics.

He led me to the dance floor amidst a barrage of whispers. I supposed it wasn't a normal occurrence for a queen to dance with the hired help.

The tempo of the baroque tune picked up and several singers added a haunting melody. Alaric pulled me close and together we formed a perfect frame. The dance was slow. Simple. *Good.* I had never excelled in dance, and many of the more intricate patterns eluded me. One of the seven sisters always ended up with bruised feet by the time we were through.

With each twist and twirl, Alaric surveyed the room, looking for threats from each face in the crowd. He hadn't looked at me once. "Do you really think anyone would be stupid enough to try something here? In front of all these people? It seems unlikely."

He came back to himself, and fixed me with a narrow-eyed stare, "Unlikely, but not impossible."

Alaric bent down on one knee as I twirled around him,

"Can't you at least *try* to relax. You'll scare all the nobles—looking at them like that."

He rewarded me with one of his rare laughs, the sound bringing a smile to my lips. "There, see? That wasn't so hard, was it?"

He flung me out, and jerked me back to him, pressing my back against his chest, "So, I've thought about what you proposed," he whispered in my ear.

What I proposed? What had I proposed?

When we were face to face again, Alaric must've noted the confusion in my expression because he explained, "Regarding myself, and Finn, and Kade."

Oh. I couldn't tell by the tone of his voice whether it was good news or bad.

In that moment, I decided I would accept his decision, no matter what it was. Kade, Finn and Alaric would always be mine, and I would always be theirs, whether we could give in to our desires and express those feelings physically or not wouldn't change that—but it would be very *very* hard not to.

"And," I prodded him, leaning in close to his ear, "What have you decided?"

He clasped my hand tighter, and I felt his Grace flow into me, projecting the longing, the lust, and the care he felt for me. "Well, it seems my sentries are terrible at following orders, and superb at finding loopholes."

I blushed.

"I—"

He shook his head, "I would be lying if I said I hadn't wanted to break my own rules. I don't blame them," he spun me around again, pulling me back, so we were hip to hip, arms crossed over each other. "So, Liana, the answer is yes."

My heart surged into a gallop, my blood rushing in my ears. *Yes?* I beheld him with something between wonder and terror.

The ball fell away until all I could see and feel was him. Alaric. *My* Alaric.

"But I have one condition," he added after a moment, and another turn about the floor—me on suddenly sloppy feet.

I snapped my head up in time with the crescendo of the song, my eyes blazing into his, and his into mine, "*I* will be the first to have you."

My legs buckled and his hand on my waist tightened to steady me, further intensifying the quake reverberating out from my core. Beyond the capacity for speech, I agreed to his condition with one terse nod of my head as the song slowed, and then stopped.

CHAPTER THIRTY-ONE

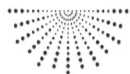

*T*hough I wouldn't be expected to produce an heir any time in the immediate future, it would have been an insult not to accept dances from the available bachelors at court. Time wore on as suiter after suiter *after suiter* implored me to dance with them. They remarked on my beauty, on the cut of my dress—one even remarked on my eye color and how it seemed to change before I remembered to keep my head down. But I didn't care.

They were courting my crown, not me. I knew *my* males had no ulterior motives. They would never accept a queen's sentry as King Consort. Kade, Finn, and Alaric would have no power. But still, they wanted me, cared for me, and would protect me at all costs. They were twice the males any of the pompous nobles were.

I had been looking forward to a break from dancing when the song ended, and turned to get myself a drink, finding Tiernan.

The Day Court emissary looked dapper in a deep blue jacket and deep grey trousers. The dark colors stressed his light hair, which he had left loose to hang about his chiseled jawline and seemed to brighten his eyes. He smiled widely, encouraging me to accept his offer to dance.

My jaw clenched. And as one, the room collectively held its breath anticipating what I'd do. There hadn't been a member of the Day Court here for an age, and I had invited one against the wishes of the council. Did I dare dance with him?

"Tiernan, I—"

He lowered his hand, "It's alright, Liana," he whispered so no one else would hear, "Someday, when there's less animosity between our courts, I *will* dance with you. I had to try," he finished with a wink, and turned to leave.

Steeling myself, I stopped Tiernan before he could walk away. The Song of Night had begun, with the sounds of drums and deep cello.

I bowed to my partner.

He registered shock for an instant before he bowed back and brought his hand up to shadow mine. Eye to eye, we moved, circling each other as a fell-cat does its prey. The dance of night was the most passionate of all dances, full of alternatingly quick and then slow movements—of pushing away and then pulling close with each beat of the drums.

The other dancers vacated the floor two by two, and the gathering of nobles stopped to watch us in raptured silence. My heart fluttered against my ribcage—a primal creature trapped in a bony cage.

Tiernan knew the dance well and lead me expertly across the floor. His hands electrified the places where they met mine and rested on my lower waist. I gasped as he lifted me into the air, spun and set me back down. I almost slipped, but he was quick to catch me, making it look as though the slip of my foot was part of the dance.

"You're an incredible dancer," I whispered to him when he pulled me near.

He put his lips next to my ear and whispered back, "I know," before he spun me out again. I shivered at the feel of his breath on my neck.

THE EFFECTS of the wine were dulling my senses, and I knew I needed to stop, but after what Alaric told me, and after that dance with Tiernan, there wasn't anyway I would make it through the evening without a little liquid assistance.

Lucky for me, there was no taster required. Everyone at the ball drank of the fountain, and no one showed any sign of having been poisoned. But just in case, either Finn or Kade held my glass for me, and always took the first sip.

"Having fun?" Finn asked me as I filled another, leaning against the wall to survey the room.

"I am," I answered him, but the truth was I was eager to have this part of the evening over with. As the queen, the nobles would expect me to remain in attendance until at least midnight, since the ball would go on until dawn. The promise of what would come afterwards was enough to make me want to flee right that moment—take Alaric by the hand and just go. I wanted him. I had wanted him almost from the first moment I saw him. And now I could have him, but I'd have to wait.

Patience was never my forte.

I filled a second glass for Finn and handed it to him, "I know I've already apologized," I began, biting my bottom lip, "But I hope you know how sorry I am for making you do something you didn't want to do. I—well—"

Finn pasted on a tight-lipped smile, "You are the queen, Liana. You don't need to apologize."

"Yes. I do. If it weren't for the pain, I wouldn't have—"

"The pain?"

He narrowed his eyes at me and I took another swallow of my wine, deciding he should know the truth, whether it seemed more an excuse than anything, "When that doorway opened, there was this pull," I told him, pointing at my chest, "Right here. And at first it was just that, a strange *pulling* sensation... but it grew stronger until it was this horrible ache. So, when you stepped in front of me, I just knew I *had* to go down there to make the aching stop. I wasn't thinking clearly, and I should've told you—"

"Your Majesty," Kade bellowed, waltzing over to the fountain where we stood. His eyes glinted with mischief. He leaned in close to my face to whisper, "What do you say we have a dance and set this place on fire?"

"She hasn't decided yet," Finn said, raising his eyebrow in challenge, "Maybe she'd rather dance with me and cover it in ice."

I would have to decide, eventually. The nobles in attendance wouldn't want to be kept waiting in suspense for much longer.

Kade and Finn continued to argue in harsh whispers at my side. Both the Graces of fire and ice were highly respected and would make my court proud, though they saw fire as the stronger of the two. But ice was known as being easier to control and would set their minds more at ease. Morgana herself burned down an entire wing of the palace when she was learning to control her one known Grace.

Before I could decide, Kade grabbed me around the waist and pulled me onto the dance floor. Finn rolled his eyes, tipped the contents of his wine down his throat and stalked from the room. He would be back.

"I hadn't decided yet," I snapped at Kade but followed him onto the floor, not wanting to cause a scene.

"And I'm not forcing you to, I just want to dance," he said innocently, smirking as he led me by the hand.

The fire awakened in my blood the moment he pulled me against him to begin the dance. I swayed under the sudden surge of power, intoxicated by the heat spreading through me.

Kade teased me with his hands, squeezing and releasing my

waist, breathing against my neck when he came close. It only coaxed the burning embers into a blaze that begged for an escape from the shackles of my skin. Then Kade spun me outward, and I caught sight of Thana hovering in one of the entryways. She wouldn't come in even though I told her she would be welcome, regardless of what the nobles thought of her attending.

Her eyes met mine from across the room and she beckoned me to go to her. That's when I noticed her flushed cheeks and the way she wrung her hands together. Something was wrong.

"Kade, I have to go."

His face screwed up into a frown, "Go? Why?"

I tipped my head toward Thana, and Kade saw what I did, "Is something wrong?" he asked me.

I shook my head, "I don't know."

Kade scanned the room, searching for Finn and Alaric, but Finn still hadn't returned, and Alaric was in heated conversation with Silas, likely to do with Ronan's execution or the missing Fae who had yet to be found.

Thana waved at me again, and turned away from the entrance, beckoning for me to follow. It could have been something as unimportant as a forgotten necklace meant to be worn with the gown. That female could make a fuss about anything with little effort.

"I should go, Kade. She probably just forgot something," I said, breaking him out of his search for assistance, "It'll only be a minute, are you coming with me?"

He pursed his lips, and I could tell he was debating whether to disturb Alaric—to let his captain know we were leaving for a moment. "Just a few minutes or Alaric will have my head."

We walked from the room arm in arm and entered the dim corridor. The flourish of Thana's off-white skirt flickered around the bend in the corridor ahead.

"Thana!" I called, and rushed to catch up to her, Kade on my heels.

We rounded the bend, and she looked back from up ahead, eyes wild and dark in the torchlight, "Hurry!" she urged us, rounding another corner, leading us towards the western wing of the palace.

"Thana, wait!" I called.

Kade and I shared a concerned look when she didn't return, before sprinting to catch up. My heel caught in a chipped tile, and Kade had to catch me before I sprawled face-first to the ground. His touch was heated and his eyes glowed yellow in the gloom, telling me his Grace was activated and at the ready should he need it.

I kept his hand in mine and felt the flames which had dwindled inside me come back to life in a great burst of warmth.

I couldn't hear her steps up ahead anymore, but there were only two places she could go. The corridor ended in a sea-side terrace, and there was only one other corridor attached to it, leading to a collection of vacant chambers.

A miasmal sensation crept over me, raising the small hairs on the back of my neck, making me shiver. Kade's jaw was set— his eyes narrowed, ready for anything.

We darted around the last bend. The moonlight spilled onto the floor from the terrace twenty paces ahead to our right. *Where was Thana?*

I looked down the corridor leading to the vacant chambers, but neither heard, nor saw anything. Kade wrapped his hand around the hilt of his sword.

"Liana, we need to go back. We'll send guards to find her."

I had been about to protest when Thana stepped from the shadows next to the terrace, the frightened expression wiped from her face. "You've already found me," she said, and I hardly recognized her voice.

"Is everything alright?" Kade asked her, his back rigid.

She walked forward, and a glint of steel flashed in her hand. A dagger. Jewels set into its silver hilt gleamed with blue and purple and red, throwing reflections against the polished tile.

"Thana? What are you doing with tha—"

"I'm sorry, Liana, but you were never meant to rule," she said, and a heaviness settled deep in my bones. My heartbeat thudded in my ears as she raised her hands.

Kade's sword fell to ground with a clatter and I turned to find him on his knees, clutching at his throat. *No.* I ran to him, falling to my knees. His eyes were wide, panicked. He couldn't breathe. His skin cooled, and then heated, and then cooled again. Thana. *Thana* was pulling the air from his lungs.

"Thana!" I screamed, my voice raw and breaking, my eyes brimming with tears at the obvious pain tightening the lines of Kade's face, "Thana stop it, he can't breathe!"

But she didn't stop. Kade's eyes bulged, and his face reddened.

"Stop, please! You're killing him," I cried.

I turned to her and found her smiling. *Smiling.*

I tightened my grip on Kade and felt the fire at my core build and burn, hotter and brighter than I had ever allowed it to be before. I swung my arm out in an arc, and the flames spilled from my fingertips in a roaring wave. She deflected them with a flick of her wrist, and they extinguished in mid-air. *No.*

With another flick of her wrist a tremendous gale crashed into me. My body left the ground. A shriek died in my throat as I collided with the stone wall, and all the breath abandoned my lungs. I gasped for air, unable to move. She had me pinned against the wall with a constant barrage of wind I couldn't fight —couldn't get free of.

I watched as Kade keeled over, his hands limp, eyes rolled back.

My heart twisted, cracking, on the verge of shattering.

"What have you done?" I shouted at her through the tears, "Let me go!"

She turned to me, releasing her hold on Kade, but my warrior didn't wake. He didn't so much as twitch.

Kade. My mind rebelled at the thought—at the possibility he wouldn't wake. Searing fury replaced the fear, and the ring on my finger pulsed.

This is a nightmare. Not real. Not *real.*

But it was real.

I'd kill her. I'd make her suffer.

"It's time for him to reclaim what's his," Thana hissed, moving closer to where I writhed against the force of her Grace.

"I trusted you," I snarled at her, looking down the corridor. Someone must have heard, there would be help coming any second. But none came, and I realized they couldn't hear. The music from the ball was too loud. Even at this distance, the drums and violin echoed against the walls.

"Stupid child," she spat, "If you had just eaten the hawthorn, there would have been no need for this. You could have died in your sleep. Peaceful. And your sentry could have lived."

Who was she? This monster before me. She was not my Thana. Not the one who nursed me back to health when I first poisoned myself with verbane berries. Not the one who chastised me for hiding in the forest instead of attending my lessons. This Thana was a stranger with eyes like a serpent and the voice of a madwoman.

"You won't get away with this."

She laughed, raising the dagger before me, now only an arms breadth away, "I already have, thanks to you. Once you drank of the water of the Sidhe, I knew *he* was right—that you were the one Morgana had chosen. All he needs is your power and he can return."

Thana eyed the ring on my finger and considered the blade in her talon-like fingers. There was a jewel missing. Four stones ran a line up its hilt, but a diamond shaped setting sat empty at the butt of the blade. "Well that, and one more thing," she said, "May you find peace, Liana."

She raised the blade.

I screamed.

A flash of movement, and then Thana was knocked to the ground. Her Grace released me, and I fell to my feet. Tiernan charged Thana again, using his Grace of earth to pull the vines from outside. They grew with vicious speed, hurtling toward Thana.

I ran to where Kade lay and rolled him onto his back. His flesh was cool to the touch, his body still. His beautiful face was pale and twisted. I felt for a pulse, for anything, *anything* that would tell me he lived.

A clattering sound had me flipping onto my back. Tiernan lay on the ground, dazed, but still alive, his arm bent at an odd angle beneath him. Thana clutched the blade in her grasp, rage glinting in her dark eyes, her teeth bared. She surged toward me, blade out, a feral battle-cry tearing from her throat.

I jumped to my feet, my pulse galloping and my body tensing. At the last second, I twisted, catching her wrist, and diverting the blade from my chest. I tightened my hold on her, gasping at the rush of power as her Grace activated another of my own.

A torrent of air roiled within me, filling me until I was near bursting. She raised her hand, but before she could use her Grace against me again, I released the violent storm from my core, driving my palm into the centre of her chest.

She catapulted backward. And I watched as sheer terror flitted across her face before she vanished from my view, falling from the edge of the terrace—her screams fading the further she plummeted, until they stopped entirely.

CHAPTER THIRTY-TWO

*R*unning footsteps rebounded through the corridor. A group of nobles came to a gasping halt when they saw me. The tears were flowing endlessly, streaming down my face and dropping onto Kade's cheeks.

He wasn't breathing. But I thought I could feel the faintest of a pulse, slow and off-kilter when I felt under his jaw.

"I need a healer!" I shouted at the nobles who were standing there, dumbstruck, not doing anything to help. Where was Alaric? Finn? I searched for their faces but couldn't find them and the hurt in my chest intensified. "Now!" I commanded, my voice straining, when none moved to get help.

A female stepped forward, knocking two nobles out of her way. She knelt on the other side of Kade, her eyes wide and hands shaking as she searched for the injury.

"He suffocated," I whimpered, "He can't die. He *can't*."

The healer placed her hands over Kade's chest, and closer her eyes, concentration drawing hard lines in her forehead. Her mouth tightened, and she removed her hands, "Not even the strongest of Graces can bring someone back from the brink of death, majesty. I'm so—"

My chest split wide open, "No," I growled at her, and grabbed her hands, forcing them back onto Kade's chest. "You will *not* give up on him."

I placed one of my hands atop the healer's and prayed to the gods that Morgana was also Graced with the ability to heal. The healer bowed her head and pushed her Grace into Kade. I did the same, digging deep within myself to find what I needed to heal him. But it wasn't a healing force I felt there. Thana's air still lingered within my core, and I felt the ring pulsate on my finger again.

Bent in concentration, I opened my palm and coaxed the air from my center, forced it to listen to my call and do my bidding. It left me in a rapid gush, and my chest contracted at the release. Kade's chest rose, his lungs filling with the air I shoved down his throat.

Then I felt it, a peaceful warmth—a calm spreading inside me. The healing Grace. I sobbed at the discovery and pressed my hands firmly against Kade, careful not to lose contact with the healer. The ability radiated through me, coursing through my fingertips and into Kade, finding and fixing. Healing. His body warmed under my palms, and his heart beat strengthened. I pushed harder. Spots danced in the peripherals of my vision. My body swayed with the effort and a cold sweat broke out over my brow.

My breaths came in ragged pants, but still I forced the energy within me to keep flowing. Kade's intake of breath was sharp and long. He choked on the air as it filled his lungs, his hand flying to his chest, clutching at his black tunic. Without thinking, I took his face into my hands and kissed him. He tensed in surprise, his skin heating in defence before he softened and pulled me against him.

The gathered nobles emitted sounds of shock and dismay. But I didn't care. Kade was alive. He would be alright. I pulled away from him amidst the echo of footfalls charging toward us.

Alaric and Finn barreled through nobles, knocking several right off their feet.

Finn raced to Kade, and seeing that his brother was awake and without physical sign of injury, he placed two gentle fingers under my chin, caressing my jaw, "What happened?"

Alaric took stock of the scene before him, and I swore I could see the relief rolling off him in waves when our eyes met. He seemed frozen, unable to move save for the shaking of his hands at his sides and the rapid rising and falling of his chest. Then his sights fell on something behind me and I heard a moan, turning to find Tiernan struggling to get to his feet.

The grating sound of steel being unsheathed was the only predecessor to Alaric's attack. He flew at the Day Court emissary with a fury beyond any I'd ever seen in his eyes. It took the last dregs of my energy to stand and put myself between him and his prey.

"Don't," I said, trying to stave off the dizziness. I clenched my fists hard enough for my nails to draw blood from the palms of my hands, "He saved my life."

The weakness in my limbs intensified, and I let my body slump back to the tile, "It was Thana," I told him, burning claws scratching up my throat, my stomach twisting in protest.

He knelt before me, a look of mortified shock crossing his features, "Where is she?"

I looked to the terrace, an image of her face as she fell, twisted in horror and pain came unbidden into my mind, "Dead," I told him, clenching my teeth against the string of her betrayal.

CHAPTER THIRTY-THREE

*M*y eyes burned from exhaustion. I'd stayed up through the rest of the night and was watching dawn break over the bay in an explosion of soft colors. My males were all with me, lounging about my bedchamber. Finn was bent in pensive focus, twirling a small blade between his thumb and forefinger. Alaric sat next to Kade, who lay in my bed, now almost fully recovered, but drained. They were deep in whispered conversation.

The room was tense with unspoken words. I hadn't wanted to talk about what happened. Every time I had to say her name, I winced, a lancing pain shooting through my heart. The palace guard had been searching for her body since the incident but had found nothing. The only explanation was she had been swallowed up by the sea, in which case, they weren't likely to find her.

I overheard a snippet of Alaric's conversation with Kade and sighed. The nobles who watched what happened had spread word of my Grace through the entire court already. They had witnessed me bring a Fae back from the brink of death with only the aid of a newly Graced, and unskilled healer. They were saying I must be the strongest healer ever known to our kind. No one could bring the dead back to life, but in their eyes, that's what I had done.

No one noticed the air I forced into Kade's lungs, and no one was there to bear witness to my use of Kade's fire. *I'm a healer*, I told myself for the umpteenth time, preparing myself to speak the lie when asked. It was too risky, Alaric said, for them to know the truth. Different is dangerous—unpredictable. And the Night Court didn't embrace change well.

"Tiernan, majesty," a servant said, entering my bedchamber after a gentle knock on the door.

I still hadn't thanked him for what he'd done. He saved my life not once, but *twice* now, and I wasn't sure how I could ever repay him for that. After Kade awoke, Finn helped him back to the royal quarters and Alaric had had to carry me back. I was too weak to walk and blinded by tears at the death of my closest friend—but more so for knowing she was never my friend at all.

Removing the blanket Finn had wrapped around my shoulders, I stood, my legs sturdier than they had been all evening, "Send him in please."

Alaric cleared his throat, running a hand through his dark hair, and stood at my side. Finn put away his blade, and Kade propped himself up on an elbow.

Tiernan entered the room with an air of uncertainty, his teeth pulling at his bottom lip, "I'm sorry for the intrusion. I wanted to see you were well."

I crossed the room in three long strides and pulled him into an embrace. He softened at my touch and loosely hugged me back, brushing the scruff on his jaw against my hair. I breathed him in, the peaceful scents of sea spray and pine bringing me a sense of calm.

"I'm alright because of you. If you hadn't found me, I'd be dead, and then so would Kade. I don't know how to thank you."

He released me, and I stepped back, finding Alaric next to me. He shook Tiernan's hand, "Thank you, Tiernan—on behalf of all of us," he said, and the newfound respect he had for the Day Court emissary was clear in each word. "We'll have to think of a way to reward you for what you did."

Tiernan inhaled deeply, pushing the hair from his face, "I have a request," he said, his eyes flitting to mine.

"Name it."

He pulled a sealed letter from his trousers and held it out. I took it into my hands, recognizing the seal of Suriel, Queen of the Day Court. I cocked my head at him, not understanding what it meant.

Tiernan sighed, gesturing at the letter, "It's a formal notice to the queen. It states I hereby relinquish all ties to the Day Court."

My pulse quickened, "What are you asking?"

He regarded me then, his gaze steady, unwavering, "I would like to be given a place here at the Night Court, as a sentry in your Royal Guard. If you'll have me."

I looked to my males for guidance, waiting for them to dispute his request, but none did. "Kade?" I asked, "What do you think?"

The giant warrior spread half-naked on my bed pursed his lips, "He saved you when I couldn't. He deserves the position—maybe more than I do."

"Don't say that," I snapped at him, earning myself a roll of his ochre eyes. I turned to Finn, "And you, what do you think?"

Finn shrugged, "I trust him. And I can't say that about most," his eyes flitted to Tiernan, whom he gave a grateful nod.

Alaric said nothing when I turned to him. He stared into my eyes as though attempting to decipher my thoughts. His brows pulled together, and then he must have seen something within me, because all at once his expression softened, and he blew out a long breath.

Alaric nodded to the emissary, "Welcome to the Royal Guard, Tiernan."

I could only imagine the uproar that inevitably would ensue when the denizens of my court found out. But they would come to accept it in time. I hoped.

CHAPTER THIRTY-FOUR

*A*laric sent Kade and Finn back to their chambers to rest and instructed Tiernan to take one of the vacant rooms next to theirs. He would have his belongings moved down tomorrow. Reluctantly, I let my males go, already anticipating when I'd see them again—afraid to let them out of my sight for even a moment.

In only a few hours, Ronan would be hanged, and both threats against me will have been eradicated. At least, both threats from within the palace walls. Thana's words repeated in my head, poisoning my thoughts with doubt. *It's time for him to reclaim what's his.*

His.

The Mad King.

The sentries Alaric sent out returned with disturbing news. They found three of the missing Fae. Dead—each stabbed in the chest, their bodies left to desiccate on the cliffside. I had a suspicion I knew who'd stabbed them and for what purpose. The Blessed Blade was not a myth. I had seen it. And it was the Mad King who intended to wield it. With the blade he could steal a Grace from any Fae he pleased. But he wanted my Graces.

I twirled the ring on my finger again, feeling its sentient pulse again. The blade wasn't complete without the dragon's eye stone. And I was willing to wager, the Mad King couldn't do what he had planned—whatever that was—without it. *Never take it off*, Morgana had told me. And so, I never would. I would die before I let it fall into his hands.

I would have to tell Alaric, eventually. But for now, I wanted him to have a reprieve from the constant worry and stress. Tomorrow. I would tell him tomorrow and we would figure it out together. The five of us. I wouldn't let anything tear us apart —never again.

We stared out into the bright dawn of a new day as it filled the sky with golden light. Alaric pulled me to him, wrapping me in his warm embrace, rubbing warmth back into my arms.

"Everything is going to be alright," he told me, and I turned to find a deep sincerity in his steady gaze.

I tried to smile. I wanted to agree with him, but knew the danger was far from over.

Alaric tucked my hair behind my ears, cupping my face in his large hand. Devotion and fear filled me as his Grace flowed from his hand into the core of my being. Slowly, he kissed me— tenderly and with so much passion my chest tightened and legs trembled.

He pulled away, but kept his forehead pressed against mine, "I'm sorry," he whispered against my lips, "I should have been there."

I hushed him with a finger pressed lightly against his mouth, "What happened wasn't your fault, or Kade's—it's mine. I should have trusted you about Thana, and I should've known something wasn't right. I just didn't want to believe it—I still don't."

"Liana—" he started, but I didn't want to talk about it anymore. I knotted my hand into his hair and pulled him to me hard and fast. His resolve broke and he kissed me hungrily, igniting something deep within. My pulse pounded and my hands hook where they clutched his back, my nails biting down into the leather of his vest.

He moaned, and my sex wetted in response, expectant. I fumbled with the clasps on his vest, and he tugged it off—baring his toned chest and abdomen. He shuddered as I ran my fingers down the length of his tan skin, emitting an animal-like sound.

Reaching lower, I tugged at the belt holding up his trousers, and he stilled, bringing his hands down to cover mine.

"Liana, wait," he said, his breaths hard and voice raspy, "We can't. I won't force you to bed me first. It was wrong of me to ask that of you," he sighed, his face reddening, "I was jealous."

I could feel the proud length of him growing beneath my hands, only the thin material of his trousers separating us. *Force me? No.* "I want you. I've wanted you since the first moment I saw you."

He licked his lips and brought my hands up to his lips, kissing each one of my fingers, making gooseflesh rise on my skin. I swallowed, trying to concentrate on breathing. The desire he'd awakened within me smoldered, and the *need* was becoming almost painful.

Gritting his teeth, Alaric tore himself away from me and dragged in a shaky breath, "You need to rest, my queen. You'll need your strength for what I intend to do to you."

Follow Liana's story in *Bound by Secret, The Queen's Consorts Book 2* - Available on Amazon.